Deena's Deception

G.S. Carr

Brown Lady Publishing

This book is for all the men and women who risked it all for the chance to create a new life for themselves. You had true grit!

Chapter One

New York City, 1875

Two yellow teeth, one brown tooth, and four completely missing.

Deena Lyon stared into the mouth of the portly man she sat next to, examining his teeth or lack thereof. His thin lips hadn't stopped moving since she asked him the hour. He prattled on and on, swaying in his seat to the rhythm of the horsecar as it traveled down Sixth Avenue. She did her best to keep the annoyance off her face and pretended to listen as she worked. The only reason she'd asked was so she could assess the value of his timepiece.

Nice clothing could be borrowed—or more likely stolen—making it an unreliable gauge of a man's wealth. But his timepiece told an experienced pickpocket like Deena everything she needed to know. Shiny, well-maintained pieces belonged to men of true means. Fellow thieves never kept such valuable items. The price they fetched was too great, and the cost of bread too high, to hold onto such items.

Deena took her time moving her left hand low across her belly. One rushed movement, and she'd displace her false arm, exposing her duplicitous behavior.

"My mother told me not to do it," the man said, his voice filled with mischievous mirth.

"But I assume you did anyway," Deena replied, encouraging his conversation. The more he spoke, lost in his memories, the easier her job became.

"Of course, I did." His fleshy chin jiggled with his laughter. "What young boy wouldn't sneak an extra cookie when presented with the perfect opportunity to do so."

She understood his sentiment. She'd been on her own, stealing to survive for so long, it was almost second nature. Passing up a perfect opportunity to nick a few coins or valuables was unthinkable. Although, in his case, this man pilfered inessential sweets.

Deena tried to take only what she needed to keep from starving to death.

"Needless to say, my mother found out. The crumbs on... Oh, dear!"

Like a blessing from the faceless all-powerful being in the sky that her old master used to tell Deena about, the trolly lurched to a stop, sending her crashing into the man's side. Taking advantage of the disruption, her hand shot out, digging into his pocket and relieving him of his coin purse. Luck seemed to be on her side today. The pouch weighed heavily in her hand.

"Well," Deena said, recovering quickly and standing. She dipped her chin to her unwitting benefactor. "I do believe this is where I must leave you. Have a lovely day."

"Oh, um, yes," he sputtered. "You do the same."

Deena was off the trolly, strolling down the street before he'd finished his farewell. Sometimes it was too easy. But she wasn't complaining, for most of the time, it wasn't. She tucked her newfound wealth into the hidden pocket she'd sewn into the skirt of her dress.

Another job done. Countless more to go.

Deena exhaled a long, worn-down breath. Rent was due. *Past* due. There would be no rest for her until she collected every cent of the unreasonable five dollars her landlord, Mr. Smith, charged for the ramshackle room in the tenement.

Why did life have to be so hard? New York City was supposed to be like the promised land Moses talked about in the Bible. The land of milk and honey. Overflowing with work and opportunities. That particular Bible story had traveled through the slave quarters of her old plantation like wildfire. It was the main reason many of them kept from spiraling into despair.

When Deena left Virginia, her heart had been full of hope. Now... Now all she dared hope for was acquiring money in a manner that didn't require her to lay on her back. She slowed her steps. There had to be more to her existence than this.

Deena stopped in front of a dressmaker's shop and examined her reflection in the window. Even on her ebony skin, dark circles under her eyes testified to how exhausted she was to anyone willing to pay attention. No one ever did.

Shallow wrinkles creased the space between her eyebrows. Permanent reminders of her constant state of stress. If this is what she looked like after living twenty-four years, Deena shuddered to imagine her appearance at forty. Her gaze trailed down to the tear in the bodice of her dress. She'd sewn it up several times since stealing the garment three years ago. Although the style was a little out of fashion, it still afforded her the ability to roam around the city without attracting much scrutiny.

The streets of the city had taught her early on that dirty, unkempt thieves were more likely to get caught. As soon as they came near members of polite society, suspicious scowls tracked their every movement.

All around her, men and women trudged along to their various destinations, blissfully unaware of the tumultuous emotional storm brewing in the woman next to them. Even if they did, how many would care enough to offer her aid?

Deena lifted her head and straightened her spine. Self-pity was for the weak. She was not a frail lady who fainted at the first sign of conflict. She would endure any obstacle life put in her path. She had to. There was no other option.

Focusing back on the task at hand, Deena continued on her way, scanning the individuals walking by. Her eyes lit up when she spotted a thin man walking toward her. His slim-fitting black frock coat and trousers molded to his frame, denoting the exceptional quality of their tailoring. In addition, his vivid sapphire silk brocade waistcoat, further touted that this was a man of means. He kept his head bent, his tall black top hat obstructing his face from Deena's view.

Wealth and timidity. The perfect mark.

Deena dipped her chin, clasped her hand over the fake one, and positioned herself to strike. She adjusted her steps, placing herself in his path. A deep whooshing breath escaped Deena's lips when the man slammed into her with more force than she'd been expecting.

His small frame was deceptive. Although thin, his body was apparently composed mainly of taut, stony muscles. Deena recovered quickly. Her hand shot from beneath the fake arm, diving into his pocket. She snatched up everything her fingers touched.

"Oh my! So sorry," she apologized in her sweetest voice. "I can be so clumsy sometimes."

"Get off me," the man growled, in a cold, snide voice. He shoved Deena away, causing her to stumble back.

She tripped on the hem on her skirt but caught herself before landing on the pavement. Nervous jolts quickened the thrum of her heartbeat. Before she even looked into the man's eyes, she knew she'd made a mistake.

Of all the people wandering the city streets, this was the one she shouldn't have crossed.

When their eyes locked, terror shriveled her stomach, then kicked it down to her toes. A long, jagged scar emerged from his hairline on the right side of his head, zigzagging across his face, cutting through his milky white left eye, before hooking around his ear and disappearing somewhere on the back of his neck.

Mean. Nefarious. Villainous. Any of those words and many more like them would be accurate descriptions of this man. She needed to put as much distance as possible between them. Right now.

Deena choked down the lump of panic lodged in her throat. She held up her hands and backed away slowly. "Pardon me. No harm done. I'll leave you to it."

A menacing snarl was the man's only response. His good eye tracked her every movement. Deena watched him watching her, as she took one step back, then another, and another. She refused to turn her back on him. He seemed like the kind of guy who not only carried a set of knives in a secret compartment in his waistcoat but never missed his target when he threw them.

After an almost never-ending stare down, the man finally whipped around and stalked away. Every bone in Deena's spine splintered, then crumbled into a pile of ash. Never in her life had she come closer to death. She was sure of it.

Deena removed her fake arm and tucked it into the hidden pocket of her skirt. She hugged herself, hunching forward and rubbing her hands up and down her arms to ward off the last frigid tendrils of fear. Perhaps it was time to bring her day to an end. She was a jittery mess. Attempting to steal from someone in such a state would only result in her making mistakes. Mr. Smith could wait a few more days for the rent. Besides, it would be better to be homeless than in prison.

Chapter Two

Deena peered through the window of the pawnbroker's shop she'd been pacing in front of for the last ten minutes. She looked again every so often to check on the happenings inside.

Benny, the shop owner, was hunched beneath the front counter, rummaging around for something. She wished he'd hurry up and rise so she could get a good look at him to gauge his mood. The tall, stocky German man always had a smile for her, but sometimes that smile couldn't be trusted.

Some days he pretended as if she were any other client, asking no questions about the procurement methods of the items she brought him. Other times he subjected her to an inquisition.

There seemed to be no particular pattern to Benny's shifting moral compass. At least none that Deena could decipher. If she could, she wouldn't be wasting time fretting about if she should bring him the day's spoils now or wait until tomorrow.

When she'd gone home, she'd seen Mr. Smith standing outside the tenement building hassling residents for rent. Most of the coin purses she'd collected today were closer to empty than full. If she wanted to placate Mr. Smith with a partial rent payment and eat this evening, she'd need to negotiate a sale with Benny.

However, due to her lily-livered reaction to Mr. Scar, in order to pay Mr. Smith the remaining balance, she'd have to make a second exchange tomorrow after she finished working. Even if Benny accepted what Deena had today, he might not be as agreeable tomorrow.

Deena stomped her foot. Enough of this. Standing outside the shop agonizing over what to do left her doing nothing at all. One day, she wouldn't have to make these kinds of decisions. She didn't know how she'd get there, but Deena couldn't imagine being an old woman still picking pockets to get by.

Somehow, she'd change her destiny.

Until then, the grumble of her stomach made the present choice clear. Pasting on her friendliest smile, Deena opened the shop door, decorated with three golden spheres painted on the pane of glass, and stepped inside.

"Hello, Benny," Deena said in her sweetest voice. "How's my favorite pawnbroker doing on this fine day?"

Benny straightened. "Hallow my darling 'Eena," he beamed in his thick German accent. His expression warm, he held his arms out wide as if he were greeting an old friend. "I am doing exceptionally vell today. How are you?"

He was in a good mood. Excellent. He'd even thrown an endearment in front of the mispronunciation of her name that she'd deemed his nickname for her.

Deena strolled to the counter. "I awoke this morning when many others did not. For that, I am grateful, and find myself in high spirits."

She held out her gloved hand, which Benny enfolded between his. Ever the gentleman, he kissed her knuckles and patted her hand twice before letting it go.

"A vonderful outlook to have. How may I help you today?"

Please, dear heavens, let this work.

Deena leaned an elbow on the counter, pouring all her charm into a grin and flutter of her lashes. "I have a few new items for you today."

"Do you seek a loan or final sale?"

"You know me, Benny. Final sale."

"Very well. Let's see what you've got."

Deena silently cheered inside, maintaining her composure on the outside. Until the money was in her hands, nothing about the transaction was guaranteed. She unhooked the velvet chatelaine bag dangling at her waist, pried it open, and upturned its contents onto the counter.

Out tumbled a gold Albert chain, a silk puff necktie, a pocket watch, and a folded piece of paper. Deena spaced the items out, moving the paper out of the way.

"This looks promising." Benny took his time examining each object one at a time.

Deena thrummed her fingers on the wooden counter while she waited. She glanced around the shop, perusing the shelves and tables covered with everything from shoes and clothing to candlesticks and silverware.

Benny kept the place organized and tidy compared to most pawnbroker shops. That was part of what compelled her to enter more than five years ago. This version of Benny—the pleasant, generally understanding man—was what kept her coming back.

She peeked at the simple gold band on his finger. Deena had never met Benny's wife. On his more exuberant days, he'd occasionally share a funny story with her about the woman he dubbed "an angel among men." Whenever he spoke of his wife, joy and admiration infused Benny's entire being.

What qualities did a woman need to possess in order to make her husband speak so highly of her? Was she as equally pleased with Benny? Did he whisper sweet words to her while they sat at home, wanting nothing more than to make her feel special?

A prick of jealousy stabbed through Deena. What would it be like to have someone cherish and love her? She'd never know. Marriages, especially happy ones, weren't meant for women like her. Tying herself to a man would be done for the sake of protection and a stable source of income.

Although tempting, the cost of such an arrangement was too great. She'd promised herself long ago she'd never again be forced to yield to the will and desires of a man. She lived for herself. Even if some days she wondered if surviving was the same as living.

Shaking off the shroud of melancholy, Deena straightened, fidgeting with the sleeves of her blouse. No point dwelling on things she couldn't change.

From the corner of her eye, the folded piece of paper caught her attention. She picked it up. Benny still examined her bounty, so she unfurled the paper, grateful for something else to focus on.

The creases where it was folded were so worn that they'd started to rip in some places. Deena studied the words searching for ones she recognized. Unfortunately, there weren't enough of them for her to guess what the paper said. She did recognize a drawing of an eagle, a portrait of a man with white hair that curled into thick rolls above his ears, and the numbers five, zero, zero, zero. None of which was helpful in figuring out what the paper said or what it was.

Asking Benny to read it for her crossed her mind, but she quickly tamped that thought down. It was probably best not to ask more from him on a day he was willing to transact with her. She folded the paper and put it back in her bag. Maybe she'd ask him later.

"I will give you five dollars for everything," Benny finally said.

"Five dollars? You can't be serious. This is a fine railroad-grade pocket watch." Deena pointed at the item in question. "They sell new for nearly seventy-five dollars. You can do better than five dollars."

"None of these items are new, 'Eena. I have to think of my margins when negotiating with customers. And let's not forget the additional liability I am assuming due to the origins of these things."

Tarnation. Deena tapped her foot, her fist planted on her hip, thinking over his offer. Should she push him? He was fleecing her, no doubt. Yet he was also doing her a favor.

"Ten dollars," she countered.

Benny hooked his thumbs beneath his suspenders, his lips pressing together.

Oh no. Deena chewed the inside of her cheek. Perhaps she'd gone too far.

"Seven. And not a penny more."

"Done."

Deena held out her trembling hand for payment. Giddiness bubbled in her chest. She'd made enough to pay half her rent and get some food and other essentials. Rarely did she allow herself the pleasure of a sweet treat, but tonight she might stop by the bakery to celebrate this small victory. Maybe life was starting to look up for her.

Suddenly, a heinous face with a jagged scar cutting through a white eye materialized in her thoughts. On second thought, maybe it was best if she laid low for a while.

Chapter Three

Ruby Creek, Dakota Territory

Dark clouds drifted across the early evening sky, blocking out the sun and promising rain. Asa Grantt limped through his wheat field, grateful for the reprieve from the oppressive summer heat. His bum leg had been giving him trouble all day. He wanted, and needed, to be at home lying down, a pillow propped beneath his knee. Making this trek to check on the crops soured his mood, but unfortunately had become a necessity as of late.

He, as well as many of the other farmers, had been having issues with someone destroying patches of their fields. The culprit had yet to be caught, although many of them had their suspicions. Asa slowed his steps, coming upon a situation he'd been hoping wouldn't exist again. A decent-sized section of his wheat was ruined. Trampled, uprooted, and broken stalks lay scattered along the ground. This was the work of a human. Animals ate what they needed and moved on.

This was purposeful sabotage.

Asa crouched down, his leg making it difficult to do so. He examined the mess for clues. There weren't any boot prints. Whoever did this had worn light footwear meant to conceal their tracks. *Hmm.* What he couldn't figure out was why?

Ruby Creek was a nice area to live in. The town was fairly built up, but not overly busy. Most of the farmers, like he and his brother Rob had been there since the beginning. They'd proved up their land last year, and now Asa wanted to focus on improving the way they operated. Maybe even expanding into horse breeding.

Disturbances like these could derail all those dreams. This was the second time in the last month someone had ruined one of his crops. It was too close to harvest time for trouble like this to be popping up. He'd just hired Johnny on as a full-time farmhand and sent word to Mrs. Milly Crenshaw that he was ready to propose marriage to Miss Pearl Wilson. Every cent from this year's harvest would be needed to keep everything going according to plan.

Asa removed his wide-brimmed straw hat and bowed his head. "Lord. I don't know what you have planned for this situation but help me be ready to walk through it all with you."

He kept his head bent a few seconds longer, then settled his hat back on his head. With renewed peace and determination, Asa struggled to rise, dusting off his pants. The sound of footsteps approaching in the distance caught his attention.

Johnny hiked over, his expression all business per usual. The young man's head for solving problems, knowledge of all things farming related, and unwavering loyalty were the main reasons Asa had hired him despite his age. But for someone who'd only recently celebrated his twentieth birthday, the boy didn't know how to have fun. All he did was work, eat, and sleep.

"Rob is on his way over," Johnny said when he was close enough to be heard.

"Thank you."

Johnny drew to a halt next to Asa. "So, what do you think?"

"You're right." Asa peered out over the field of golden wheat, swaying in the gentle breeze. "Someone's tampering with the crops, but there's not much we can do about it until we know who it is."

Johnny tipped his hat back, revealing more of his curly midnight hair, and scratched his head. "I can do a few more patrols at night if you want."

"No. You work hard enough as is. We'll figure something else out."

"Well, I'll clean this up while you go talk to Rob."

"Thank you." Asa gave Johnny's shoulder two firm pats. "If you don't get it all done before the sun goes down, don't worry about it."

Johnny nodded. "Yes, boss."

"You have a good night."

"You too, boss."

A sharp pain shot up Asa's leg when he took a step to leave. He did his best to hide his wince. One sign of weakness and Johnny would take it upon himself to complete all the chores so that Asa could rest. He couldn't have the poor boy working himself to death on his conscience. Asa straightened, held his head high, and took careful steps to conceal his limp as he headed home.

***

Asa opened the front door of his modest three-bedroom home and nearly sighed in relief.

It was time to put his pride on the shelf. He was going to have to start taking the buggy out to the fields for a while. Else he might pass out from the pain in his leg along the way home and become buzzard food. SaraGrace would never forgive him for leaving her, even if it was to be with the Lord.

"Papa!" the little girl in question hollered from the kitchen.

SaraGrace released the spoon mid-stir in the pot of stew, hopped from her stool, and bounded over to him. She launched herself at him with the unwavering faith of a daughter who knew her father would catch her. Asa cradled her to his chest, humbled and awestruck by her unconditional love. He carried her to the sofa, keeping the hisses of pain from slipping past his lips.

"Hello, my lovebug," he said, kissing her forehead. He ruffled her silky chestnut hair, earning a gleeful giggle.

Mrs. Paty, his longtime neighbor and friend, exited the kitchen, wiping her hands on her apron. "*¡Qué linda!* Don't you two make the cutest pair? Just alike, all the way down to your beautiful blue eyes and the freckles on your noses," she crooned in her elegant Spanish accent. The corners of her light brown eyes crinkled.

Tucking SaraGrace into the crook of his arm, Asa removed his hat, then smiled and nodded at Mrs. Paty. "Good evening, Mrs. Paty. Thank you again for watching over SaraGrace for me. I hope she wasn't too much trouble."

"Your little girl was an angel as always. It is my pleasure to take care of her."

After his wife Billie ran off three years ago, not long after SaraGrace's first birthday, Asa had no clue what to do with a baby. Between trying to divide his time between planting and harvesting, building a new wooden home to replace their old sod house, and trying to figure out what to feed a red-face screaming youngster, he was drowning in anxiety and fear.

Newly widowed, Mrs. Paty had taken mercy on him, volunteering to care for SaraGrace while he worked around the farm. Every time he tried to pay her, she refused, stating that her husband had left her with more than enough money to live out the rest of her days comfortably. And taking care of SaraGrace had saved her from the crippling sadness of losing the love of her life.

"One of these days, Mrs. Paty, you're going to let me repay you for all you've done for us."

"Nonsense. My reward is in heaven, and that's good enough for me."

The door burst open before Asa could respond. His younger brother Rob sauntered into the house, full of unblemished youthful exuberance.

"Something sure smells good," he said, sniffing the air like a bloodhound who'd caught the scent of nearby prey. "What fine dish have you prepared for supper tonight, Mrs. Paty?"

"*Estofado de pollo y papas*. I used my great-grandmother's recipe. You are going to love it."

Asa shook his head. "You have to stop spoiling us, Mrs. Paty."

"Hold up, speak for yourself," Rob cut in. He walked over to Mrs. Paty, took her hand, and kissed her knuckles. "You can spoil me as much as you like, Mrs. Paty. I'm never going to turn away the affections of a pretty lady like yourself."

Mrs. Paty was twice his age, and her love for her former husband had yet to waver, but all five feet two inches of her blushed a delicate shade of red. Asa covered his mouth with his fist to refrain from laughing. Rob could charm the venom out of a rattlesnake. A quality Asa admired, and slightly envied, about his brother.

Mrs. Paty pinched Rob's cheeks. "I will always spoil you, *mijo*," she said, her eyes alight with affection.

"That's what I like to hear."

"I like when Mrs. Paty spoils me too," SaraGrace chimed in, her broad smile showing off her missing front tooth. "Sometimes, she lets me dip my finger in the honey jar and lick it off."

Mrs. Paty placed her hands on her slender hips and raised an eyebrow at the little girl. "That's supposed to be our little secret, *mija*."

"Oops. Sorry." SaraGrace dipped her chin, her cheeks turning a cute shade of pink.

Asa winked at his daughter. "I like to dip my finger in the honey jar sometimes too."

Her eyes went wide with wonder, her little mouth forming a round "O." "You do, Papa?"

"Yes, indeed. Your old man loves a treat like anyone else."

"I have a treat for you! Mrs. Paty and I made cobbler. I'll go set the table." SaraGrace climbed off the sofa and scampered back into the kitchen.

Everyone chuckled, watching the spitfire go.

"I'll go help her," Mrs. Paty said, trailing after the little girl.

Rob moseyed over and plopped down in the seat SaraGrace had vacated. "Let me know if I can be of assistance. I always be here whenever you need me," he said to Mrs. Paty

"Oh, you." Mrs. Paty shook a finger at him, but her giddy grin stole the sting from her rebuke.

Asa stretched out his leg and massaged his aching muscles. "One of these days, you'll have to stop carrying on like a shameless flirt. Else you won't be able to find a respectable bride who'll put up with you."

"If you haven't noticed, pickings for eligible ladies are slim in these parts. I'm waiting to see how your mail-order bride turns out before I toss my hat in that ring. I've heard some frightening stories. Women saying they're buxom beauties, but when they turn up at a man's door, they're so unattractive they could bluff a buzzard off a meat wagon." Rob stared straight ahead, his eyes taking on a far-off look. He shuddered at the horrifying visual his imagination had conjured.

"There is more to a good woman than just her appearance."

Despite his censure, Asa couldn't argue too much with what Rob had said. He'd heard the tales. Seen the warnings in the paper. But when one's choices were severely limited, sacrifices had to be made. Asa would take a woman from trustworthy, hardworking stock over an attractive woman who could barely stitch a shirt any day.

"That might be true, but I'm only a flesh and blood man. If I have to stay with one woman for the rest of my life, I want to have something decent to look at."

Asa shook his head. Knowing Rob, he was only half kidding, if at all. "Sorry to tell you, brother, but Mrs. Crenshaw only helps men with upstanding moral character. She wouldn't find you a bride even if you were the last man left in the Dakota Territory."

"I beg to differ." Rob laced his hands behind his head, a smug smile on his handsome face. "I'm a man made of exceptional moral fiber. Mrs. Crenshaw would love me as soon as she saw me."

"Umm-hmm. A very elastic fiber."

They both chuckled.

Rob shrugged, accepting Asa's assessment of his character. "Well, we might get to test that theory. If these disturbances keep happening on everyone's farms, we might end up being the last men left in Ruby Creek."

Asa sobered, remembering the state of his field. "It's definitely getting worse. First, it was missing eggs, dead chickens, sections of my barbed wire fences cut. Now they destroyed a good section of my wheat last night. Whoever *they* are. And I have a feeling this is just the beginning."

"Some of the others are speculating that this is the Indians. They think they're coming off the reservation and harassing us to scare us off our land."

"I don't believe it." Asa sat forward, resting his elbows on his thighs. He mulled over that bit of information, searching for the flaws and merit. It didn't matter how he felt. It mattered whether it was true or not. "We've never had problems with them before. Why would they pick a fight now?"

Rob scratched his chin, his eyebrows drawn together, contemplating the possibilities. "Beats me. And I'm not saying I believe it. Just relaying what I've been hearing."

"Either way, someone is trying to stir up fear. We have to figure out who. We can't afford to have a bad harvest this year."

"Agreed. We'll get to the bottom of this." Rob gave Asa a curt nod, affirming his commitment to solving the detrimental mystery. He sat back and slung his arm over the back of the sofa, his expression becoming playful once again. "In the meantime, back to this business about your blushing bride. Have you received a response to your telegraph marriage proposal?"

A warm flush crept up Asa's neck, all the way to the top of his ears. It had taken a whole lot of convincing and a revelation from the Almighty himself to make Asa comfortable with the idea of engaging a mail-order bride agency to help him find a wife. SaraGrace needed a mother, and he couldn't keep imposing on Mrs. Paty to be her caregiver. Not to mention all the other ways Mrs. Patty helped around the house. Cleaning, cooking, and so much more.

Initially, Rob had been one of the main supporters of Asa's chosen path to matrimonial bliss. Now he took every opportunity he could to poke fun at the way things were progressing. Asa dropped his gaze to the ground and fidgeted in his seat. Rob laughed outright at his discomfort.

"Laugh all you like. It is a very respectable undertaking. Sam worked with Mrs. Crenshaw, and she helped him find Rebecca."

"Rebecca is a wonderful lady. Treats Sam like a king. Can't argue with that."

"Exactly. And to your question, Mrs. Crenshaw said she would get back to me as soon as she speaks with Pearl."

"Well, I can't wait to meet my new sister-in-law." The amusement faded from Rob's tone. He gripped Asa's shoulder, his expression sincere. "You deserve the happiness a good woman brings. I hope Pearl is everything you hope for and more."

"I just need a good mother for SaraGrace and a helpmate around the farm. That's all I'm hoping for."

"Like I'd ever believe that's all you're dreaming of. I know you better than that. Don't worry. Pearl is going to be a lovely woman with a good sense of humor, beauty, and the patience of an angel. She'll have to be, to put up with all your grumpiness."

"I'm not grumpy," he grumbled.

"If you say so."

Mrs. Paty walked back into the living room, wiping her hands on her apron. "Who's ready to eat?"

"That would be me," Rob said, rising and heading over to the table. "Smells delicious. You ladies did a wonderful job. Can't wait to tuck into this meal."

Asa stood, grateful some of the pain in his leg had subsided. He hobbled over to the table, ready to enjoy a meal with his family. Rob was right. He did hope for more. In the secret part of his heart, he hoped for someone to love and cherish him. Someone with whom he could share his dreams for the future so that they could build them together. A partner to share his life with. But such women didn't exist for men like him. Men who weren't whole, or handsome, or charming. So, he'd settle for whoever would have him.

Chapter Four

"Deena! Deena! Deena Lyon, I know you hear me."

Deena cringed. The sound of her name spoken as a sensual purr by the smoky feminine voice made her quicken her steps. The last time Beatrice had corned her, she'd barely escaped being forcefully dragged into Mahogany House. Working in a brothel, especially that one, held no appeal to Deena. Unfortunately, the tenacious madam refused to believe her.

"Got ya," Beatrice said in a sing-song tone like they were children playing a game of hide-and-seek. Her long, elegant fingers clamped around Deena's wrist. She quickly wove her arm through Deena's, locking them together and hindering any chance of escape. "Morning, Deena. How are you today? Such lovely weather we're having, isn't it."

She spoke as if they were two old friends meeting for a morning stroll, instead of an unwilling hostage and captor. Her poignant floral scent assaulted Deena's nose, the smell so strong she could taste it. Left with no other choice, Deena slowed her steps to match Beatrice's unhurried pace.

"Morning, Beatrice," Deena mumbled. "I'm surviving. Don't have much of time to talk. I've got a lot to do today."

If Beatrice noticed the stiffness in Deena's posture, or the pull on their connected arms as she attempted to pry herself free, she didn't show it. The pleasant smile on her painted lips never wavered. "Where were you headed? Maybe I can join you."

"Just here and there. I'm sure you have better things to do than follow me around."

"How about I accompany you for a little while? We can part ways when the time is right."

"Sure. That would be lovely."

Beatrice's sweet tone didn't fool Deena. Her question wasn't actually a request. It was a command that they both knew Deena wouldn't dare refuse. A woman didn't become one of the most well know madams in New York City without acquiring some unsavory acquaintances. Ones she never hesitated to call upon when she wanted things to go her way.

"I heard Mr. Smith has been standing outside the tenement building, trying to shake people down for rent. Were you able to pay this month?"

"I paid him some. I'll be able to pay the rest shortly. I had a good day yesterday, but I needed to take care of a few other obligations first."

"You know I'll always have a place for you at the house if you're ever looking for work." Beatrice stroked Deena's forearm like a doting guardian concerned about the welfare of their beloved charge. "And it will be so much easier than deceptively relieving rich men of their valuables."

Deena kept her focus trained straight ahead. It was never wise to look a master manipulator in the eyes. They'd spot a weakness and devise a plan to exploit it before your lashes closed in a single blink. "I've never been afraid of hard work."

"Yet another thing I admire about you. But why struggle when you don't have to?" Beatrice stroked the side of Deena's face with the back of her soft hand. "With features like yours and that gorgeous, smooth dark brown complexion, you could be one of my top girls."

"Thank you for the compliment, but my answer is still no."

Beatrice's eyes narrowed, a spark of irritation flickering across them. "Starvation and homelessness have a way of tearing down the pride of even the strongest willed person," she said, her tone sharp.

"That's true, so it's a good thing I'm not there yet." Deena came to stop and finally yanked her arm from Beatrice's unrelenting grasp. She offered a too-sweet smile, strained with derision. "If I ever do find myself so impoverished, I'll let you know. In the meantime, if you'll excuse me, I need to get going."

"Very well, then. You know where to find me when you're ready. Until next time." Beatrice swept her scrutinizing gaze over Deena one last time, then strolled off in the direction they'd come.

"Have a good day."

Deena almost wanted to spit at her. She hadn't missed the subtle surety in Beatrice's voice, that there would indeed come a day when she'd become one of her harlots. Death would be a better alternative to being one of the girls at Mahogany House. But what got under Deena's skin the most was that underneath her bravado, a small part of her wasn't entirely sure Beatrice was wrong. If her life continued down its current path, Deena didn't know what kinds of depravities she would stoop to in order to survive. She'd never thought she'd end up being a petty street thief, but hunger had a way of making a person reason away their moral standards. The price of rent and food was increasing, the Metropolitan Police were gaining more authority, and her job wasn't getting any easier.

No! She couldn't give in to such thoughts. She had to continue fighting her demons, both inner and outer, until she breathed her last.

Shaking off the cloud that always accompanied a run-in with Beatrice, Deena squared her shoulders and marched on. She had work to do and no time to waste fretting over futures that might never happen.

***

Overcrowding. Horrible living conditions. Astronomical prices for basic living expenses. There were so many reasons for a person to hate living in New York City. But for each one, Deena had also had a reason to love it. Her favorite being the architecture. Elaborately designed brick and stone buildings reached toward the heavens. Each one was an exquisite example of true craftsmanship. No such grand buildings could be found anywhere near the rural plantation where she'd grown up.

Deena walked along the sidewalk, heading south on Broadway, marveling at the buildings. Some were five stories tall, occupied by various shops selling everything from clothing, to toys, and jewelry. In the distance, the steeple of Trinity Church peeked above the surrounding properties.

She should be surveying the surrounding crowd for an easy target from whom to pilfer a few items that would fetch a good price. Not ambling along like someone who didn't have a crushing financial burden weighing on their shoulders. Before she could chastise herself too much, a commotion started up behind her. Men and women shouting in displeasure, mingled with the sounds of fast-approaching footsteps.

"That's her," a man sneered. "That's the woman who stole from me."

Deena froze. There was something familiar about that menacing gruff voice. She glanced over her shoulder and every function of her body came to a grinding halt. Her heart stopped beating. Her lungs stopped drawing in air. And her legs stopped moving, failing in their duty of carrying her away from the blatant danger headed in her direction.

It was Scar! The man with the dead, white eye and scar that ran across his face, whom she'd robbed yesterday. He had another equally terrifying and even larger man with him. They picked up their pace, sprinting and knocking innocent pedestrians out of the way in their haste to ensnare her.

"You're dead," Deena's victim-turned-assailant snarled.

His abrasive threat broke through the haze of terror, keeping Deena immobile. She did an about-face and took off running. The fabric of her skirt swished about her ankles, bunching and hampering her from racing ahead at full speed. She gathered the bulky material, hiking it nearly to her knees.

Gasps rose from the bystanders who made no attempt to detain the men chasing her. No doubt, they were more outraged by the indecency of a woman exposing her bare legs than the fact that two sinister-looking men pursued her. Clearly, with the intent to inflict injury.

"Pardon me. Please move. Out of the way," Deena shouted, dodging through the individuals she ran past.

"You won't get away. When I catch you, I'm going to wring your neck."

They were gaining on her. Deena didn't glance back, but the ominous threat came from right behind her. Digging deep within her reserve of strength, she forced herself to run faster.

Dear Lord, if you are there, please help me. I'm not ready to die today! I swear I'll never steal again.

Deena swallowed, the action causing her burning throat to throb. She needed a plan of escape. She had to think. How could she get these men off her trail?

Straight ahead, she spotted the sign for Cedar Street. If she took a left on Cedar, it would take her to Trinity Place, from which she could get to Thames Street. There was a perfect restaurant tucked away on Thames that most people didn't notice unless they knew what to look for. Making it there would be her best chance at giving them the slip.

Changing course, Deena made a hard left, diving headlong into the tide of carriages, trollies, and horses traveling up and down the busy road. Coachmen shouted and cursed her stupidity, demanding she move out of the way or be trampled. Thankfully, she made it across the street without coming to harm, although there were many close calls.

Cedar Street quickly ended, bringing Trinity Place within view. She'd arrive at her refuge in no time. *Don't look back. Eyes forward and keep running.* Wise words. Ones she should have heeded. Deena glanced over her shoulder.

Her heart shriveled and rattled down into the black void where her hope used to reside. Large hands reached out and grabbed the back of her skirt. She weaved to the left, avoiding the goon's grasp. Unfortunately, her luck didn't last long. Scar came up on her right and rammed his shoulder into the side of her body, knocking Deena into the wall of a building.

The side of her head smacked against the brick surface with a sickening crack. Everything went dark, then slowly faded back into focus, white dots flickering before her blurry vision. Before she could reorient herself, two pairs of calloused hands clamped down on her arms with bruising force.

"Let go of me, you brutes!" Deena shrieked. She thrashed about like a wild animal, but it only served to make the men tighten their hold.

The men dragged her from the sidewalk, down a deserted side street the devil himself must have conjured for them to exact their hideous revenge. Refusing to give up, Deena screamed until her throat stung, then screamed some more.

No one came to her aid. Individuals walking nearby changed their course, some crossing the street, others turning around completely to avoid the disturbance unfolding before them.

Deena's entire body trembled, and hot tears stung the back of her eyes.

These men were so fiendish, they'd brazenly abducted her off the street in broad daylight. Men like that didn't fear consequences because life had taught them that there were none. At least none that they couldn't bribe, lie or kill their way out of.

They were barely off the main road and hardly out of view when one of the men slammed Deena's back against a wall, knocking the breath from her lungs. Scar leaned in, bringing his face so close to hers that their noses nearly touched. Each of his hot breaths blanketed the small space between them. Deena turned her head to the side to avoid inhaling the overwhelming stench of tobacco and alcohol.

"Do you know who I am?" Scar sneered.

Deena shook her head. It was all her aching lungs would allow her to do.

"Pete Bloodlow. And you stole something from me that I want back."

All the blood drained to Deena's feet, then evaporated from her body. Her eyes went round with terror.

The corner of Bloodlow's mouth curled into something akin to a grin, but ten times more terrifying. "So, you've heard of me." It was more a statement than a question.

It took a special kind of degenerate to strike terror in the hearts of others with just their name. Pete Bloodlow was such a man. Deena's entire body trembled like a withering leaf in a gusty autumn breeze. She'd stolen from the Grim Reaper himself. A man who brought death and destruction wherever he went. There had yet to be a person alive who'd crossed Pete Bloodlow and lived to tell about it. Deena was of the mind that she wouldn't be the first.

"Yesterday, you stole a..."

"I'm sorry. So sorry," Deena whimpered. "Please, please, please have mercy."

Deena begged without shame. If there was a possibility that she could make him feel a scarp of sympathy, she had to try. She no longer had anything to bargain with. Everything she'd stolen from him had been sold. Perhaps she could convince Benny to give it back. *How* she didn't know. The money had already been spent.

"Yesterday, you stole a piece of paper from me," he growled above her whimpering.

"A piece of paper?" Deena repeated, a bit too shocked to fully comprehend what he was talking about.

"Yes. I want it back."

Deena took several deep breaths, trying to calm down enough to remember everything that happened in Benny's shop. Her life depended on it. Had she seen a piece of paper among the other items? She squeezed her eyes shut, visualizing the countertop.

Her eyes popped back open, and for the first time since seeing Bloodlow's face again today, she felt a glimmer of relief. "Yes. I have the paper. I can get it to you. I know where it is."

"Hey now," someone shouted from the entrance to the ally. "What are you two doing to that woman?"

Deena and her two captors turned their heads to look at the newcomer.

To her relief, not just one, but three men stood at the entrance of the alley. For once, someone had decided they wouldn't keep walking. For once, someone decided to help her. Deena sobbed, hot, joyful tears spilling freely down her face. She'd never been more grateful to another human being in her life.

The man at the front of her rescue group gripped a baseball bat. His crouched stance indicated he wasn't afraid to use it.

"Do you know who I..."

In a last-ditch effort to survive another day, Deena tossed a right hook, connecting with Bloodlow's chin. His head snapped back, and his grip loosened.

"Help me. Please help," Deena screamed.

Needing no other provocation, the three men charged down the alley, attacking Bloodlow and his crony. Their hands fell away from Deena. Not wasting time, Deena ducked beneath the fray of swinging fists and weapons and ran for her life. Continuing with her original plan, she ran to Trinity Place, took a left then continued to Thames Street.

Deena never slowed her steps, even when she saw the restaurant that she planned to make her hideout for the next hour or so. Hoping for a better outcome than the last time, she chanced a look over her shoulder. No one followed her. Her legs wobbled, weakened by the surge of relief.

"Thank you!" she cried out with her face lifted to the sky.

She ran on, not stopping until she reached her destination. Yanking open the door to the restaurant, she slipped inside and restrained herself from collapsing into an incoherent mass of blubbering relief. Although just barely.

Chapter Five

Deena slouched in her chair and loosened the bonnet ribbons beneath her chin. Her elevated body temperature, galloping heartbeat, and restlessness made it hard to stay seated without squirming. She jumped every time another patron scraped their fork across their plate too loudly or set their cup down with a thud.

Shortly after sitting down, a young serving girl in a simple navy-blue dress and crisp white apron strolled over to the table. Her pleasant, genuine smile helped to allay some of Deena's anxiousness.

"Good day, miss. What'll you have?"

"Tea, please," Deena replied, returning the girl's smile. She didn't need to peruse the menu. She couldn't really afford the tea, but she couldn't sit here without purchasing something.

"Coming right up." The girl dipped her chin in a short bow, then ambled away to fulfill her order.

Deena scanned the cozy interior of the dining establishment. A handful of square tables were arranged in two neat rows and adorned with pressed white linen tablecloths, polished silverware, and folded cloth napkins. Paintings of families picnicking in the park, beautiful landscapes, and other lovely scenes hung on the walls, illuminated by the natural light streaming in through the large front windows.

Two women sat directly behind Deena, tittering with excitement about someone's impending nuptials. A group of men were a few tables away, talking and laughing amongst themselves. Overall, none of the other customers had taken notice of Deena. They were all too absorbed in their conversations.

That realization helped Deena to relax further. She'd done it. At least for now, she'd escaped the infamous Pete Bloodlow without losing any limbs or her life. Her next challenge would be figuring out how to make the getaway permanent.

Bloodlow owned the streets of New York City. His networks of thugs stretched from Harlem all the way across the East River to Brooklyn. He counted former members of the Daybreak Boys and the Bowery Boys as some of the top leaders in his gang. Even the Whyos gang steered clear of him.

Deena wiped the sheen of sweat from her forehead and chin. If she were going to get clear of Bloodlow, she'd have to leave New York and probably the entire East Coast.

The serving girl came back before Deena could spiral too far down into the chasm of despair. "Here you go, miss." She placed in front of Deena a white teacup trimmed with silver along the base and handle, then tipped the teapot, pouring the steaming golden brown liquid into the cup.

Deena forced a smile. "Thank you."

"Will you be needing anything else?"

"No, that will be all for now."

"Please let me know if that changes."

Deena nodded. It was all she could do to keep from shouting at the girl to leave her be. Fearing for one's life made it hard to devote much energy to the niceties of polite society. But the girl had a rather pleasant disposition and was only doing her job.

Deena reached for the tea. Her fingers shook so hard the liquid sloshed in the cup, almost spilling over the brim. She closed her eyes and took several calming breaths.

Don't lose your head. There is a solution.

She'd figure her way out of this somehow. She always did.

To her dismay, the blathering of the two women behind her grew louder. Deena couldn't think over their noisy conversation. She leaned back in her chair, listening for the perfect moment to interrupt and tell them that the volume at which they conducted their dialogue was rude.

"Again, thank you so much for this wonderful news, Mrs. Crenshaw," the younger woman said.

"As I've said before, please call me Milly. And I am more than happy to tell Asa you'll be along in two months. I'm sure he will be more than understanding."

"I do hope so. He is such a wonderful man. I've been carrying some of his letters around with me in my reticule. If my grandmother weren't so sick, I'd come straight away. I hear the Dakota Territory is lovely in a wild, rustic sort of way. A land with plenty of opportunities. Asa and his brother have done quite well for themselves. Oh dear, I'm rambling." The younger woman paused, no doubt blushing, or doing something of the like. "Please excuse me. That's what happens when I'm excited."

"No problem at all, dear. Seeing you this pleased affirms why I started my Matrimonial Agency in the first place. The Lord set me on this path to help young women like you find good men that will provide for their families. Men that you can be delighted to wed. I'm glad I'm able to carry out that mission through you and Asa."

"Thank you, Milly. I truly mean that. You are..."

The rest of their exchange faded into a low buzz on the edge of Deena's consciousness. From what she could piece together, there was a man named Asa in the Dakota Territory waiting on a woman to come wed him. They must have one of those correspondence-courtships Deena had heard about. Men and women were putting ads in the paper, or engaging agencies, to help them find spouses. Never meeting and only communicating through letters until they agreed to marry.

A new plan began to form in Deena's mind. What if she pretended to be the bride? She'd have two months to lay low out West. That would keep her well out of Bloodlow's reach and give her plenty of time to formulate a plan for the rest of her life. Maybe she'd continue west out to California.

As the woman had said, the West was supposed to be a land of opportunity. *Like the North was supposed to be after colored people got their freedom*. Deena scoffed at the cynical thought. Life in the North had proven to be nothing but hard work for little to no pay and with few opportunities to better one's circumstances.

But perhaps this time, it really could be different. She'd have a man taking care of her, temporarily eliminating her need to worry about money. She could spend her time learning a trade. Save enough to start her life over. When she left, she'd be equipped to find a respectable job wherever she ended up.

The more Deena thought about it, the more appealing the idea became.

What about the marriage bed?

Deena grimaced into her tea at the thought. She drummed her fingernails on the side of the teacup, brooding over this new shortfall in her plan.

Asa would have certain expectations of his wife, same as any other man. There was no way she'd be able to honor those expectations. But she could make him *think* she had. Valerian root was the basis of a wonderful sleeping draught. One she could use on the nights he wished to exercise his rights as a husband. In the morning, she'd pretend their night involved matrimonial intimacy. It was a brilliant idea.

Deena lifted her chin and took a confident, steady sip of her tea. She was going out West. She's been wanting to leave New York City for a while now. This wasn't the push she'd envisioned, but it was the push that she needed to take hold of her destiny finally.

Now all she had to do was get her hands on those letters, which should be easy enough. Relieving a woman of her reticule was almost second nature at this point. Then she could find someone to read them and tell her where Asa lived. She'd send him a telegraph stating there'd been a change of plans and that she was ready to come to him now. All he had to do was pay the fare for her travel.

What about your promise not to steal?

Deena groaned. Leave it to her conscience to choose the most inopportune moment to remind her of her hastily made promise in the heat of desperation. She'd requested for God to help her escape Bloodlow, which he had, for now. Holding up her end of the bargain meant refraining from stealing. Which meant she couldn't assume this woman's identity.

Or perhaps, God was still working to make her escape permanent. What if he was presenting her with this opportunity to take the other woman's place as a mail-order bride? To fully free her from Bloodlow's terror? And she wasn't actually *stealing* anything. She was merely pretending to be someone else for a short while. Carrying out an act the other woman already intended to do.

So, she wasn't actually going back on her promise.

This was her chance at a new life. She'd be a fool not to take it. A slow smile built on Deena's lips. Each passing second increased her excitement. She shifted slightly in her chair so that she could fully see the two women.

Oh, yes. This would be all too easy.

Chapter Six

Asa adjusted the tilt of his hat, checked the collar and top button of his best shirt, and tugged on the lapels of his jacket. He hadn't been this nervous in a long time. Picking up his future wife from the train depot was turning into a bigger test of bravery than he'd imagined. Working out in the fields with Johnny under the blaze of the summer sun would have been a more enjoyable experience than this. He paced up and down the platform, alternating between shoving his hands in his pockets, hanging them at his side, and folding them behind his back.

When Pearl had sent a telegram saying she no longer had to wait the two months for her grandmother and could come immediately, Asa's heartbeat had taken off like a stampede of wild buffalo. A litany of questions plagued his mind. Would she like it in Ruby Creek? Would she be a good mother to SaraGrace? Would she consider him adequate as a man and husband?

He wasn't delusional enough to want anything like love. But he didn't want Pearl to find life on the farm to be miserable, either. Asa couldn't take another wife leaving him and SaraGrace behind because she hated what he could, or more so couldn't, provide. He'd try his best to make sure Pearl enjoyed the life they shared together.

The train carrying his intended approached the station, its shrill whistle piercing the air. He fussed over his appearance one last time before the train came to a stop. Men and women poured from the open car doors, their expressions both weary and eager to have reached their final destination.

Asa pulled the piece of paper with Pearl's name from his pocket and held it in the air. He hoped she saw it because he didn't know what she looked like. All he knew was that she had dark brown eyes and curly raven hair. She'd once asked if he wanted to exchange photographs, but he'd declined. It was cowardly, and looking back, he should have consented to it. At the time, the thought of Pearl receiving his picture and ending their correspondence because she found his scarred face repulsive had kept him from agreeing to the trade.

Several women matching the rather vague description wandered around the small wooden platform searching for those who'd come to collect them. One or two glanced at him and his sign, but none came over. Asa continued to scan the area.

A beautiful colored woman strolled in his direction, capturing his full attention. He quickly averted his gaze and turned in the opposite direction. Staring at a woman, no matter how attractive he found her, as he waited for his intended was disrespectful to both women.

"Pardon me. Are you Asa Grantt?"

Asa spun back around and faced the woman who'd been walking towards him. Her full, heart-shaped lips parted, gracing him with a warm smile. One of her bottom front teeth was a little crooked, adding a perfectly imperfect charm to it. Combined with her smooth, dark mahogany skin, round, upturned eyes, and delicate features, the woman exuded the type of beauty poets tried to immortalize within their verses. She looked up at the sign in his hand, then back at his face.

"Pearl?" Asa asked with hope and dread in his suddenly gruff voice.

Admittedly, he hadn't expected his mail-order bride to be a woman of color, but he wasn't upset that she was. This woman was exquisite. Too much so for her to agree to marry him. He should have sent her a picture to save himself from paying to bring her here, only to have to pay to return her once she rejected him.

"Umm-hmm. That's me," she said, her voice a little too cheerful. Her gaze fell away from his. "But my friends call me Deena. Long story, but please call me by that name."

Deena? The haze of enchantment ebbed away, suspicion taking its place. She'd never mentioned this alternate name in any of her letters. He watched more closely, noting when she scratched the back of her hand. Years spent surviving on the battlefield during the War among States had left him with a keen knack for spotting the agitated signals of a liar.

"Deena," he said slowly, trying out the name. It suited her much better than Pearl. Another reason his wariness peaked.

She rocked from the balls of her feet to her heels, her smile waning. Breaking the awkward silence that descended between them, she said, "Yes, exactly. It is a pleasure to meet you finally. I was overjoyed when I received your offer of marriage." She reached into her traveling bag and pulled out a stack of envelopes. "I've carried around the letters we've written for a long while now."

Asa examined the envelopes she held out to him. Sure enough, there was his handwriting scribbled across the wrinkled, beige paper. Rob's chiding voice rang in his ears, "Don't mess this up, brother. Stop sabotaging yourself." That was exactly what he was doing. Making up ridiculous excuses to send this exquisite woman away before she rejected him. But if the Lord had deemed him worthy of binding his life to this woman, then who was he to argue that he wasn't?

Pearl—or Deena—might not have seen his face before this, but he'd laid out clearly the man he was in his letters. That was what won whatever affection she had toward him. So far, she didn't seem repulsed by the motif of scars crisscrossing over his forehead and cheek on the right side of his face. Her jitteriness probably had more to do with traveling thousands of miles to marry a man she'd never met than any nefarious scheme. Why would a woman move her life from New York to the Dakota Territory and lie about being his prospective bride? The absurdity of that notion squelched the last traces of his unfounded mistrust.

Asa pasted on his best attempt at a reassuring smile. Remembering his manners, he removed his hat. "I was glad to hear that you accepted. I've enjoyed getting to know you, as well. Welcome to Ruby Creek."

"Thank you."

"Here, let me get that for you." He extracted the small bag from her delicate hands, surprised to find her resistant at first. "Do you have any other luggage?"

"Nope, this is it. I don't have much."

Made sense. She'd been a schoolmarm in a small town, the name of which he couldn't recall. Without the support of her family, she probably wouldn't have survived on her salary. And taking care of an ailing grandparent could prove costly. He slung her bag over his shoulder, then began walking out of the train depot. Deena strolled silently by his side.

"So, your grandmother made a speedy recovery?" he asked as a way of making conversation.

"Yes, she did. My parents and I were overjoyed that she did."

"Parents?" Asa quirked an eyebrow at Deena. "I thought your father died when you were a young girl."

"Right. Yes. My father is dead," she stammered. "But... um... Sometimes it is hard for me to think of him as gone. I feel like he's always with me."

"Understood."

When he and Rob lost their parents to consumption ten years ago, he wouldn't allow himself to believe they were gone at first. Now they were the tranquil undertone of his heart's rhythm.

"I hope you don't mind, but until we say our vows, I've asked a family friend, Mrs. Paty Hinojosa, if she would host you in her home. She is a widow with a plot of land not far from my farm. Her husband proved it up before he died, so she owns it free and clear. She said she'd be happy to have you."

"That sounds wonderful. I'll have to think of a way to thank her."

"Maybe you can bake her one of those red bean pies you told me about. I wouldn't object to you making one for me and SaraGrace, either."

The corner of his lips curled into a playful grin. A whim he didn't give into often but wanted to try to do more for Deena's sake. Unfortunately, she didn't seem inclined to join in his mirth. Her gaze left his yet again and bounced around their surroundings.

"Yes," she replied, a nervous lilt to her voice. "I'll have to do that."

"She invited us over for supper this evening. There will be a few other people. My brother Robert—we call him Rob—and some friends of mine who wanted to welcome you to town."

"That sounds like a lovely evening. Can't wait."

Now that was a bald-faced lie, which Asa couldn't brush aside. Her pinched expression, the way she dragged her feet and held her stomach as if she were in pain, spoke volumes about her anticipation for the evening's events. An offer to decline Mrs. Paty's invitation teetered on the edge of his tongue, but Asa refrained from speaking the words aloud. Mrs. Paty had put a lot of effort into preparing the food and cleaning up her home. And he really wanted Deena to meet his friends. The faster she built a rapport with people, the easier it would be for this place to feel like home to her.

Asa placed Deena's bag in the bed of the buckboard, then came around the side to help her into the seat. He gripped the reins and set the horse off at a steady trot. They settled into a comfortable silence, each lost in their thoughts.

This was it. He was on his way to being a married man again. If nothing went wrong in the meantime.

Chapter Seven

Was this real?

Deena sat quietly, observing the people around the table, asking herself that question for the umpteenth time. Everyone was so warm and welcoming. Their uninhibited laughter and joking filled the small house as if despite the hard work they endured every day, they considered themselves blessed and were grateful to wake up each morning.

The woman named Alice had pulled Deena into a hearty hug after introducing herself. She sat on Deena's right, next to her husband, Jonathan. Asa was at the head of the table across from Rob, with SaraGrace on his left, and their host Mrs. Paty next to her. It was a tight squeeze at the table clearly not meant for so many guests, but no one complained.

It had been years since Deena had been at a gathering brimming with so much affection and camaraderie. No one plotting against anyone else. No veiled deception. Only a small group of friends enjoying each other's company.

"Mrs. Paty," Rob said, tipping his chair on its back legs and patting his flat stomach. "That was de-li-cious. Green beans, mashed potatoes and gravy, soda biscuits, and fried side pork. You outdid yourself today."

"Thank you, *mijo*. I'm glad you liked it."

"Yes, ma'am, I did. The only reason I didn't lick my plate is because I am trying to make a good impression on my future sister-in-law." He winked at Deena.

Deena wiped the napkin over her lips to hide her grin. She liked Rob. She sensed that he was a flirt by nature, but he meant no harm. His strong square jaw, high cheekbones, twinkling sky-blue eyes, sandy blond hair, and other classically handsome features probably made him a favorite among the town's women. She couldn't deny he was nice to look at, but she didn't see him as anything other than the spirited, fun-loving brother she'd wished she had growing up.

"And how about you, *querida*?" Mrs. Paty looked at Deena, her eyes brimming with hopeful expectation. "Are you enjoying the meal?"

Luckily, Deena didn't need to lie when she said, "Yes, ma'am. Everything was wonderful."

"Good." Mrs. Paty sat a little straighter in her chair, her wide smile growing broader.

No one had cared about Deena's opinion in a long time. It felt nice to know that her praise mattered to someone.

"I liked the food too," SaraGrace beamed. "Mrs. Paty cooks real good."

"Thank you, *mija*." Mrs. Paty bent and kissed the little girl's cheek.

SaraGrace smiled so hard her cheeks pushed up, making her eyes squint. She happily dove back into her plate, showing Mrs. Paty how much she enjoyed the food.

"So, Pearl, tell me about your life in New York," Alice said. "Asa said you're from the rural part, but did you make it into New York City from time to time? Did the ladies walk around wearing all them fancy dresses from Paris?"

"Call me Deena," she replied.

"Oh, that's right. Sorry about that. Where did that nickname come from if you don't mind me asking?"

Deena pushed some of her potatoes around on her plate. How did she answer that question? What was a good excuse? "Pearl is my grandmother's name. My mother let me pick what they called me when I was younger, so me and Gran weren't always looking up when she called me. I don't know where I heard it, but I liked the name Deena, so they let me use it."

"Thought your grandmother's name was Martha," Asa asked. His eyes narrowed on Deena ever so slightly.

The low hum in the pit of her stomach started up again, the same as it had when she'd seen him at the train depot. Where Rob was light and joyful, Asa was dark and shrewd. He watched everything. Deena could sense the way he absorbed every detail of what was happening, storing it away for another time.

"Martha is her middle name. When I picked my new name, she decided she wanted a new one too. Neither of us were fond of the name we were born with, so I guess I should retire the tradition of passing on the name Pearl if I have a daughter."

Something Deena couldn't quite name flashed across Asa's eyes. His demeanor softened, and he nodded, satisfied with her answer. He must have memorized every letter he and Pearl had exchanged. She'd have to be more careful in the future. There had only been four letters between Asa and Pearl in the reticule she'd stolen. Those must have been Pearl's favorites because they weren't in sequential order. There were just enough details in the letters for Deena to have basic knowledge of the other woman, so she'd have to stay away from specifics about her life.

Deena shoved an ample scoop of mashed potatoes into her mouth, hoping someone would fill the silence and steer them away from Alice's question about her life in New York.

"My family has a tradition of naming the first boy 'Byron,'" Jonathan chimed in. "Me and Alice put a stop to that. It's my middle name, and I can't stand it. I'm only trying to pass on things my boys can be proud of."

"Ain't that the truth," Rob said with a chuckle. "That's why you stuck it out in the wilderness with us. Once your land is proved up next year, you'll have a wonderful legacy to leave your boys."

Jonathan grunted. "If we make it to next year. With these Indian attacks happening on everyone's farms, we might have to split in order to save our hides."

"Oh, hush up that kind of talk," Alice admonished her husband. "You're jabbering about nonsense. No one is going to run us off our land. Besides, you don't even know if it's the Indians."

"Yes, I do." Jonathan pushed back his chair and stalked over to his coat, which hung on a peg next to the door. He dug inside the pocket and pulled out a strap of leather with three feathers attached to it. Coming back to the table, he flung the item in the middle of the table and pointed a condemning finger at it. "See here. That's an Indian headband. Proof it was them. Found it on my property when some of my crops were ruined a few nights ago."

Deena reached for the headdress, stopping right before touching it. "May I?"

"Sure."

She gently picked up the sacred accessory and examined it. "This wasn't made by an Indian."

"How can you tell?" Asa asked. He regarded her with his intense curiosity. Elbows on the table, he leaned forward as if entranced by what she'd say next.

"Feathers are sacred to Indians. They have meaning. Each tribe is different, but the Indians of the plains generally use the feathers of Great Horned Owls and eagles. These are turkey feathers. Whoever left this on your property was trying to make it look like Indians attacked you, but they didn't know enough about them to make it realistic."

"Impressive. How do you know all this?" Asa asked.

A warm flush spread over her cheeks. She must be going a little crazy because something akin to delight spread through her at the pride in his voice. She knew a plethora of random facts. Deena wanted to regurgitate them all to keep him enthralled by her knowledge.

"An old acquaintance liked to travel all over the world. He was fascinated with different cultures and would tell me stories about the people he met on his journeys."

Asa crossed his well-muscled arms over his chest and nodded. "That's some useful information. As Jonathan said, we've been having some issues recently with someone tampering with our crops and stirring up trouble. I planned on doing a little investigating. Would you care to assist me?"

"I'd be honored."

"My goodness," Rob interjected. He slapped the table. "If this is the kind of woman Mrs. Crenshaw is digging up at her agency, then sign me up. I'll take a bride right now."

"No comment," Jonathan replied.

"Good idea, sugar," Alice said, playfully scowling at her husband.

Asa shook his head. "Please excuse my brother. He was born without manners."

All the adults laughed. In her own world, SaraGrace hummed to herself while she ate, oblivious to the discussion happening around her. When the laughter subsided, Jonathan steered the conversation in a new direction. Alice and Rob yammered on with him, Mrs. Paty occasionally weighing in.

Deena eased back in her chair, happy to enjoy the conversation without participating. She peered through her lashes at Asa, taking in her temporary future husband. Like Rob, he had a strong square jaw, but his features were rugged where his brothers were more delicate. His dark cobalt-blue eyes shone with astute intelligence. He was the kind of man who took his responsibilities seriously and believed in hard work.

He ran his hand, calloused from working in the fields, through his dark honey-blond hair. Apart from the smattering of scars running along his forehead and cheek, his face was perfect. Deena noticed the way he tried to keep the right side of his face angled away from her. No doubt to hide the scars he thought diminished his attractiveness. In truth, she didn't mind them. Pearl's letters had mentioned that he'd been in the war, which was probably where he got them. To Deena, they spoke to his strength and will to survive, giving him an air of courageousness. One she found very appealing.

As if sensing her stare, Asa glanced up. Their eyes met, and the corner of his mouth lifted in an amiable grin. Deena quickly looked away, her chest tightening, and took a sip of her coffee. Guilt speared her yet again. From what she could tell, Asa was a good man. His friends and family were good people. They didn't deserve to be lied to. She was a horrible person and shouldn't be here. She should come clean right now and grovel for their forgiveness.

An image of Pete Bloodlow's murderous face came to mind, keeping her lips clamped shut. Maybe she wouldn't stay the full two months, but at least for now, she'd be a fool to tell them anything. She needed to create a plan for how to move on. And fast.

Chapter Eight

Deena sat up in the small, reasonably comfortable bed in the room Mrs. Paty had given her last night for the duration of her stay. Legs tucked to her chest and chin resting on her bent knees, she stared at the bare wooden wall in front of her. What next? She was here in the Dakota Territory. Her initial meeting with Asa and his friends had gone well. And she didn't have to worry about Bloodlow finding her.

When she'd decided to come, fear of the imminent threat to her life had shut down all her mental faculties except those dedicated to survival and fleeing. Now she needed to think long and hard about where she wanted her final destination to be, and how she would support herself financially once she arrived. She had to learn a trade. But what? Washerwoman? Domestic servant? No doubt, Asa would teach her about farming during her time with him.

Maybe she could find a way to put those skills to use.

She straightened when a new thought came to mind. When Bloodlow had apprehended her, he'd mentioned wanting a piece of paper. He'd come all the way back to where they'd bumped into each other to hunt her down personally. Whatever the paper was, it must be valuable. Deena leaned over the side of the bed and took hold of her travel bag. Hauling it into her lap, she rummaged around in it until she found the item in question. She held up the folded square of parchment, scrutinizing it in the early morning light pouring through the room's single window.

This was what she almost died for. The reason she had to flee her home. Such a deceptively insignificant-looking object had cost her everything.

Shaking her head, Deena unfolded the paper and laid it flat on her blanket. She examined the paper, trying and failing to make sense of it. She ran her hands over the rough surface, smoothing out the wrinkles as if that would help her read what was written across the page. To figure out why it was so important.

It didn't.

Days like today, she wanted to curse the world she'd been born into and the way she'd grown up. To blame Mark, her old master's son, and the invisible collar he'd fastened around her neck. He'd kept her blind to her own ignorance, and how he was training her to be dependent upon him. His "exceptional favorite pet," he used to call her.

Deena stared at the piece of paper a little longer. It was no use. The words didn't suddenly make sense. She didn't miraculously learn how to read. Although, she did think the numbers five, zero, zero, zero were more meaningful now. Together those numbers made five-thousand if she remembered correctly. If it had such a large number on it, surely this was something valuable. But what exactly was it?

A knock sounded on the bedroom door. Deena started. She quickly stuffed the paper back in her bag. "Yes?" she called through the door. She cleared her throat, removing the last remnants of sleepy scratchiness. "Who's there?"

"*Buenos dias, querida.* Asa has come for you. I made biscuits, bacon, and eggs if you wish to eat before you leave. There is also fresh coffee."

Asa has come for me?

What did that mean? They said she'd stay with Mrs. Paty until she and Asa wed. Did this mean he wished to do so today? Deena hopped off the bed and padded to the door on bare feet. She looked down at herself. Continuing the conversation through the wooden barrier would be rude but answering the door while dressed in nothing but a threadbare nightgown could be equally offensive if Mrs. Paty were a woman of delicate sensibilities. Although, something told her she wasn't.

Deena stood behind the door, using it to shield herself while she opened it a crack. Mrs. Paty's warm smile greeted her on the other side.

"Ah, I see I've caught you unawares."

"Please pardon my state of undress. I thought it rude to make you shout through the door."

Mrs. Paty laughed softly. "Don't worry. I understand."

"May I ask if you know what Asa's intentions are for the day? So that I know how to dress."

"I believe he wishes to show you around the farm. He'll most likely teach you the chores that need tending."

Deena nodded. "I see. Please give him my apologies. I'll be ready shortly."

"I'll let him know."

Deena waited until Mrs. Paty walked away before closing the door. She slumped against the wood, expelling a quick huff. Her gaze roamed back to the bag atop her bed.

That paper was her ticket out of the Dakota Territory and, more importantly, out of Bloodlow's reach. She could sense it. She had to find someone to read the paper. And the sooner, the better.

***

Asa sipped his coffee, listening to Mrs. Paty recount a memory from her childhood in Monterrey, Mexico. He loved her stories about her family and how close she was with her four siblings. Rob was a great brother, and Asa loved him unconditionally, but it would have been nice to have another brother or sister or two around while growing up.

Light footsteps captured his attention. Asa peered over his shoulder, careful to angle his face so that the bad side was obstructed. Deena entered the kitchen in a simple pale-yellow dress, cinched at the waist by a white apron tied into a small bow on her lower back. The sunny color reflected off her rich brown skin, giving it a lovely radiance. Her long lashes fluttered down, sweeping her cheeks.

"Good morning," Deena said, her bright smile trained on him.

Asa nodded. "Morning."

"Please excuse my lateness. I wasn't expecting you to visit so early."

He guffawed, raising a teasing eyebrow at her. "What farm girl doesn't know that chores start at the crack of the day?"

"I'm not..." Deena closed her mouth, apparently thinking better of whatever she was about to say. "You're very right. Tomorrow I'll be ready before you arrive."

"Don't believe her," Mrs. Paty said with a mischievous smirk. "Whether she grew up on a farm or not, she's an eastern girl. No one from the east works as hard as us Homesteaders. Her early is our mid-day."

Asa and Mrs. Paty laughed at her accurate assessment of nearly all the newcomers to life in the west. When Asa had first moved to the Dakota Territory, he never could have imagined how hard he'd have to work to prove up his land and construct a new life for his family. But the hard work only made the triumph that much sweeter.

"You may very well be right about that, Mrs. Paty," Deena said, her tone pleasant.

"Well, if you two will excuse me, I'll go check on SaraGrace. Please help yourselves to anything you'd like." She gave Asa's arm a good-natured pat, then strode from the room, leaving them alone.

Asa took another sip of coffee, stealing a moment to appreciate his future bride silently. Her beauty both thrilled and terrified him. Luckily, he now had more to offer a wife financially than he'd had during his first marriage. Hopefully, that would be enough to make her stay.

"I was thinking that after we finish working, I can take you into town so you can get some personal items. I don't have much in the way of things a woman needs. And I noticed you only had one bag when you came, which means you didn't bring much with you. We can get you some brushes, a hand mirror, and a few new dresses and whatnot. Maybe a new wardrobe."

"You're too kind, but I can't let you spend that much money on me."

"Why not? You'll be my wife soon. A man has to take care of his family."

Deena nibbled her bottom lip, her forehead creased with worry. Did she not believe he could afford to provide her with the necessities?

"Perhaps we can discuss it further once we finish with whatever tasks you wish for me to do."

"Very well then," Asa agreed, although he had no intention of letting her refuse his offer. Whatever she needed, he would provide. "SaraGrace will stay with Mrs. Paty today so I can teach you everything without interruption."

"Alright."

"Shall we be on our way then? Daylights a wasting."

"Yes. Let's." Deena turned and headed out of the kitchen.

Asa made to follow her but stopped when a realization hit. She hadn't eaten anything. He grabbed a cloth napkin from the table and filled it with a few biscuits and pieces of bacon. No time like the present to start proving he'd always try his best to take care of her.

Chapter Nine

What would it be like to be a chicken? To run freely with little worries. Oblivious to the eventuality of ending up in the frying pan.

A strange set of thoughts, yes, but ones that struck Deena as she spread dry feed throughout the hencoop. Was it better to be like them? Not knowing a threat lurked in the darkness, waiting to lash out and douse the flames of life.

The birds flocked around her feet, pecking at the ground, solely focused on feeding themselves. They either didn't notice, or didn't care, that Asa ransacked their nests and took their eggs. What would it feel like to be so unburdened by anxiety?

Asa emerged from the henhouse, his large hands filled with freshly laid eggs. "Feeding the chickens and collecting the eggs should generally be done first thing in the morning. Even before you milk the cow. If their eggs aren't collected early enough, Big Jen tends to get a little cranky once you finally do come around." He pointed at one of the larger hens strutting by Deena's feet. "She's the barrel-chested one with the dark brown streak running down her back."

"Collect the eggs first. Will do."

Deena added that information to the list of instructions Asa had given her. Her list of responsibilities now included milking the cow, fetching water, tending the family garden, preparing food, and of course, collecting eggs and feeding the chickens. How he managed to get all that done before she'd arrived was a mystery.

"Thanks." Asa jutted his chin toward the house. "Let's get these eggs inside, and then I can take you into town."

Deena followed him toward the house. Although he didn't complain and tried to move with even steps, he walked at a much slower pace than earlier this morning, and his limp was much more defined. Deena was a lot of things, but callous wasn't one of them.

Sympathy tugged on her heart, making her want to do something to assist him. Only the strain at the corners of his mouth, and the beads of sweat running down the sides of his face as he fought to keep himself steady and his expression neutral, stopped her from telling him to sling his arm over her shoulder and lean on her.

Asa was a man of principle. She had no doubt about that. If he wanted to be the stoic leader, she'd let him be that. Their time together wouldn't be long enough for her to demand that he make changes to his lifestyle. Even if they were for his own good.

"Why did you answer the call to 'tame the western wilderness?'" Deena asked, striking up a conversation.

"Like many young, foolish men, the adventure of it all called to me. Plus, I was married to Billie at the time, and we both thought it would be the perfect chance for us to create something of our own. Our marriage wasn't doing so great at the time and I thought starting over somewhere new would be good for us. That was over six years ago. It's been hard, and it didn't help our marriage, but I wouldn't have done anything differently."

Curiosity about the entire story between Asa and his previous wife nipped at Deena, begging her to ask him about it. What had caused their divorce? Had she left, or had she died? One of his letters to Pearl had mentioned Billie, but only as a declaration that he'd once been married. No other details were given.

Deena couldn't risk asking a question about something he'd already discussed with the real Pearl. Maybe she should search through the house for the letters Pearl had sent him. They might give her more insight into the topics they'd discussed. Of course, that would mean finding someone to read them. Thus leading to her having to explain why she needed said person to read the letters *she'd* written.

She smiled at Asa. "You've done very well for yourself out here. That's something to be proud of."

"Thank you. Now that you'll be here to help with the household responsibilities, I want to work with Johnny on a plan to expand the farm's operations. I'm thinking about breeding Friesian horses. They're a handsome breed. And there is always a need for good horseflesh."

"That sounds like a grand idea."

Hands full of eggs, Asa juggled them around until he could open the door for her. Deena passed, entering the house, and gave him a small closed-lip smile. A pang of guilt sliced through her. Hopefully, it wouldn't be long between her departure and Pearl's arrival. She didn't want to add "hindering his hopes and dreams" to the list of ills she'd committed against him.

Asa quickly deposited the eggs in a bowl and covered them with salt. "I probably shouldn't ask this of the woman I'm supposed to be wooing, but what about you? Why did you agree to come out here and marry me?"

"Well, I... um..."

"You mentioned feeling like a burden to your mother, especially with the expenses she's been incurring paying a doctor to tend your grandmother. But if I might be so forward, now that I've seen you, I have a hard time believing you'd have trouble finding a husband in New York."

Scratching the back of her hand, Deena mulled over her response. She had no idea how Pearl would answer that question. Did that even matter? The only way she could answer was with her truth. Well, a form of it. "I grew up loved. My parents doted on me and tried their best to give me opportunities that many in our situation didn't have."

"Were you born a slave?"

"Yes. Our master was good to us. He treated us so well that when the government granted us our freedom, we decided to stay. His son Mark was a few years older than me. He let me follow him around everywhere he went. He taught me so many things. Expanded the way I saw the world. To me, he was the older brother I'd always wanted, and I was too naive to know to stay away from him." She looked down at her feet. "Around my sixteenth birthday, he tried to hurt me. I fought back and escaped."

That wasn't completely true. She'd fought back, but Mark had won that battle. The frenzied look in his eyes, the smell of his sweat, and the horrible sound of his grunts would forever be burned on her soul. That was the first time she'd ever experienced true terror in her entire life.

She'd been running from that feeling ever since.

"Is he the one who told you about his trips around the world and what he'd learned while traveling?"

"Yes. Mark was an explorer." Deena couldn't keep the respect out of her voice. "It was one of the many things I admired about him. His betrayal cut me to my soul. After that incident, I... my family and I left Virginia and moved up North, chasing a chance at prosperity. We didn't find what we were looking for."

"I'm sorry to hear that."

Deena shrugged. "That's the truth for many freed slaves. All we can do is make the best of our situation and try to thrive anyway. Which I guess is why learning that you were looking for a bride made me think that maybe, I'd been looking for my opportunity in the wrong place. I was tired of being afraid. I wanted to try something different. *Be* someone different."

"I understand that feeling."

Asa nodded slowly, the crease between his eyebrows deepening. He took a step toward her, then stopped. He looked torn about something he wanted to do. Like he wanted to give her comfort in some way. He listened so intently to her that Deena could almost imagine he was taking her pain into himself.

He stuck his hands in his pockets as if that were the only way to keep from touching her. "I'll admit I want to hug you, but it wouldn't be right. We should get going. It's a decent ride into town, and Mr. Tucker likes to close up the general store early on Thursdays to go play poker at the saloon."

Deena smiled to herself. She appreciated the sentiment and his boldness of telling her how he felt. "I'm ready. Let's go."

She followed Asa to his buggy. He helped her up into the seat with ease. Her hand lingered in his, their attentions absorbed with each other, silently passing words of comfort and encouragement. He gave her hand a gentle squeeze, then walked over to the other side.

Another nail sank into the coffin of Deena's dying resolve to continue lying to Asa. Why did he have to be such a good man?

Asa set the horses at a steady trot. "Before I forget, I wanted to talk to you about something."

"Sure. What is it?"

"I don't want to pressure you into doing anything you're not ready for, but I was hoping we could get married soon. That way, we're not imposing on Mrs. Paty for too long. And when you're settled in my house, I was hoping you could start teaching SaraGrace her numbers and how to read."

Deena stared out at the expanse of lush greenery surrounding them, nibbling on her bottom lip. Her mouth soured, and her stomach rolled in protest.

Tell him. Tell him the truth.

"I... I'd be honored."

"Good. We just got a new missionary in town not too long ago. I forget his name. He's watching over the church while our permanent Reverend is traveling. I will talk to him while you get what you need. Hopefully, he can marry us within the week."

Within the week?

Deena's heart pounded against her ribs. So soon? It shouldn't cause her to panic. This is what she knew would happen. The moment she'd prepared for since leaving New York. So why did it suddenly feel like the sky and ground raced toward each other, threatening to crush her between their collision?

Chapter Ten

Deena stepped through the door that Asa held open for her into a quaint, well-decorated dressmaker's shop. Bolts of fabric in an array of different colors were stacked along the back wall. To the left, a curtain concealed a changing area, which was flanked on each side by two mannequins wearing premade dresses. Tucked in the back-right corner, there was a small platform set in front of a full-length mirror. Beautiful green patterned wallpaper decorated the walls, adding a touch of welcoming sophistication, and a crystal chandelier hung from the ceiling. Deena imagined this was what a nice dressmaker's shop in London or Paris looked like.

"Asa! Deena! Lovely seeing the two of you again so soon," Alice greeted them. She was crouched next to a dressmaker's model draped in a periwinkle-blue gown, with a needle and thread in one hand, and the hem of the dress in her the other.

"Afternoon, Alice." Asa lifted his hat. "How are you doing?"

"I'm breathing, so I have nothing to complain about. What can I do for you today?"

"I was hoping you could help Deena get a few items. Dresses, nightgowns, and lady underthings." Asa blushed, his cheeks and neck turning a light shade of red. "Whatever she needs, I'll pay for."

Alice stood. Hands on her hips and a wide grin on her face, she eyed Deena from head to toe. "Of course, I can help with that."

"Thank you so much. I need to run over and talk with the missionary. I'm hoping he can marry us within the week." Asa turned to Deena. "I'll be back to pick you up in a few."

She nodded. "If I get done before you, I'll come to find you."

"Sounds good. Alice, take real good care of my lady," he said in a teasing tone.

"I will, don't you worry."

Asa winked at Deena, then left. She blinked several times, watching his retreating figure. He wanted her to have everything she needed down to her "under things". Not that she would accept all of it, but it still left her bewildered by the way he so freely gave what was his.

Shaking her head, Deena looked at Alice. "I know he said I could get whatever I want, but I don't feel right taking that much from him."

Alice tilted her head, studying Deena. "Why not? He'll be your husband soon. Part of his job is taking care of you."

"I know, I know. He keeps saying the same thing." Deena dug the toe of her shoe into the ground. "But I still don't feel right about taking so much so soon."

"I hear you." Alice's features softened with understanding. She rubbed a gentle hand up Deena's arm. "It's hard being able to let yourself need someone else. Being vulnerable takes time and practice."

Deena gave her an appreciative smile. "Thank you."

"How about we start you with two day dresses, some drawers, a nightgown, nightcap, and... oh, and a nice dress for your wedding day."

"No dress for my wedding."

"Why not? You have to have something nice for your special day."

"I just…"

"Accept it. I'm not letting you walk out of here without one."

"Fine. Since you're twisting my arm I'll accept it. Just make sure the dress isn't too nice."

"Hogwash. I am going to make you the prettiest dress anyone's ever seen this side of the Mississippi. Now step up here, so I can get your measurements." Alice pointed to the platform in front of the mirror.

Deena took sluggish steps in protest but did as Alice said. She kept her expression that of someone being coerced into a task they'd much rather avoid, although secretly excitement bubbled inside her. The dresses in the shop were gorgeous. She couldn't wait to see what lacy confection Alice created for her.

Alice removed the measuring tape from around her neck and tapped on Deena's arms, indicating she needed to lift them. Again, Deena did as instructed. Alice went to work sliding the tape across her body, never writing the measurements down.

"So, do you own this shop?"

"Yes, ma'am, I do. After Jonathan proved up our land, and it started turning a profit, we saved up our money and invested in this shop."

"How long have you been a seamstress?"

"For long as I can remember. When I was little, I used to take the extra cloth from my mama's dresses and stitch together little rag dolls for myself. My mama and grandmama were both seamstresses. The best in the state of Georgia. Guess it runs in our blood."

"You have a talent, no doubt about that. Those dresses are beautiful," Deena said, pointing at the two gowns next to the dressing room.

"Thank you. I love what I do, and I think that's what makes the difference."

"I wish I had a gift like that. I can barely stitch a shirt without poking myself or sewing a finger into the garment."

"Getting a bunch of children to behave and listen while you teach is a real gift. One I wish I had." They both laughed. "If I could get my children to do their chores the first time I asked, I would have much fewer gray hairs." Alice pointed to the patch of gray hair at her temple.

"Working with children does have its challenges," Deena replied. Not that she would know.

"If you ever want to learn to sew, let me know. I'd be more than happy to teach you."

A refusal danced on the tip of Deena's tongue. She'd taken enough from these people.

She didn't want to impose any more than she already had. Although learning to be a seamstress could prove valuable when she moved on.

"I think I might take you up on that offer."

"Anytime you're ready. You can bring SaraGrace with you when you come. Susan and J.J. would love to play with her."

"I'll let you know."

Alice gently squeezed Deena's arm. "I've got your measurements. I will get the dress for your wedding done first. Everything else should be done in a few weeks."

Deena gave her a wobbly smile. "Much appreciated."

Another pang of guilt sliced through her. If all went well, she'd be gone in a few weeks. Which meant she was now adding to Alice's workload and making Asa pay for clothing she'd never wear. Unless she decided to wait until the dresses were done. Then she could take them with her.

Yeah, but then you'd be stealing from Asa.

It wasn't stealing if he gave them to her as as a gift. But that was splitting hairs. Something she seemed to be doing a lot of lately. Deena tried to remember Pearl's figure. The other woman was a little wider and much better endowed in her bosom. The dresses wouldn't fit if Deena left them for her. Either way, there was no way she could come out of this situation without more dirt on her hands.

Unless you tell the truth.

"This may sound like a strange question," Deena said, her tone hesitant. She twisted her skirt around her finger. "Have you ever told a lie so big it started to weigh on you? And you wanted to tell the truth but doing so might have put you in a worse situation."

"I have."

"What did you do?"

"I told the truth," Alice said matter-of-factly, her hands on her hips.

"Oh." Deena dipped her head, shame setting her face aflame.

Alice let her hands fall to her sides, her shoulders slouching. "Now, that was a simple answer, but the reality is a lot more complicated. It took me a while before I got to the place where I could tell the truth. I had to realize that nothing I do is beyond forgiveness if I am truly repentant. And even if the person I wronged didn't forgive me, the Lord did. That is enough for me."

"Those are wise words and very good advice. You know, I feel like we could be good friends. I haven't had one of those in a very long time."

Alice drew her into a tight embrace. "I would like that very much."

They held each other for a moment, each taking and giving support, in the promise of a budding friendship. Deena gave Alice one last squeeze before pulling apart.

"Well, I better get going. Since we're done, I'll go find Asa."

"Make sure to tell me the specific date you two settle on for the wedding. I'll have your dress finished by then."

"I will. Thank you again."

"Take care now."

"You too."

Alice walked Deena to the door. She left the dress shop feeling both lighter and heavier. Alice was right. She needed to tell the truth. But she couldn't. Not yet.

***

"All done," Asa said as he finished tying a ribbon around the braid he'd put in SaraGrace's hair. Two on each side of her head, the way she liked it. He handed her the nightcap, which she quickly put on, stuffing the braids beneath it.

"Thank you, Papa."

"You're welcome, my lovebug. Are you ready to say your prayers?"

"Not yet." SaraGrace ran out of her bedroom without further explanation.

Asa followed behind, curious about what she was up to. She darted through the house toward the kitchen. The pitter-patter of her little feet came to an abrupt halt.

"You're gonna be my new mama, right?" SaraGrace asked Deena before Asa could stop her.

He peeked through the entryway and found his daughter gazing up at Deena, patiently waiting for an answer. Deena regarded SaraGrace, her jaw slack, as shocked by the question as he was. Water dripped down from her motionless hands, hovering over the washbasin where she'd been cleaning the dishes from supper.

"Um. Yes, I suppose I am," Deena finally said.

"Then, you should come to say your prayers with me and Papa."

"I don't want to intrude on your time with your father."

"You're going to be my mama, which makes you family. Papa says that families have to say their prayers together before they go to bed. So that means you have to come pray with us."

Deena smiled affectionately at SaraGrace. "That makes perfect sense."

Deena dried her hands on her apron and SaraGrace held out her hand. Deena hesitated, then took it and allowed the little girl to drag her along. Asa headed back to the room before either of them noticed him observing their exchange. He sat on the bed and folded his hands in his lap as if he'd been sitting there the entire time, waiting for them to return.

His heart expanded, crowing its excitement. For the first time in a long time, he was hopeful. It would take more time for Deena and SaraGrace to bond fully, but so far, they were doing great together. At first, he'd only wanted someone to take care of SaraGrace. Now he envisioned a true mother-daughter relationship, filled with love between them.

Thank you, Lord.

"My new mama is gonna pray with us," SaraGrace announced, marching into the room with Deena in tow.

"That sounds like a great idea."

SaraGrace released Deena's hand, bounced over to her small bed, and crouched onto her knees. Deena did the same. Asa struggled into a kneeling position next to SaraGrace. They rested their elbows on the bed, folded their hands, and bowed their heads. Deena glanced at the two of them, something akin to uncertainty in her expression. Asa gave her a reassuring smile, raising his folded hands in a silent invitation to mimic him. Deena matched his posture and bowed her head.

"SaraGrace, would you like to go first?" he asked.

"Yes, Papa. Dear Lord, thank you for sending me a new mama. I've wanted one for a long time. I hope she stays. She seems like a nice lady. Maybe Papa can teach her how to do my hair. Thank you for loving me and thank you for Papa loving me too. Amen."

"Amen," Asa said, uplifted by his daughter's prayer. "Deena, would you like to go next?"

"Um... I'm a little out of practice. What am I supposed to do?"

That was odd. In her letters, she'd mentioned going to church every Sunday. Maybe she didn't pray much on her own outside of church service. It wasn't his place to judge. At least she was willing to learn and participate with them.

"All you have to do is talk about whatever is on your heart. What you're grateful for. What you're worried about. Anything."

"Very well." Deena bowed her head, but kept her eyes open. "Dear Lord, thank you for bringing me to Asa and SaraGrace. They have treated me better than I deserve. I'm sorry for the lies I've told. Please forgive me. Amen."

The lies she's told? Odd, but then again everyone has lied about something at some point. Perhaps she was making a sweeping prayer to cover her general daily transgressions.

"Amen. My turn. Dear Lord, you are such a wonderful provider. You've given me so much and continue to bless me. Please continue to watch after Pe... Deena and SaraGrace. Protect them when I can't. And dear Lord, please help put an end to the attacks against the farmers. Amen."

"Amen," SaraGrace and Deena repeated.

SaraGrace scuttled into her bed and lay on her side, her folded hands placed beneath her head. Asa pulled the blanket up to her neck and tucked it around her. Deena stood beside him, holding her middle as if protecting herself.

SaraGrace smiled up at them. "Goodnight, Papa. Goodnight, New Mama."

"Goodnight," they replied in unison.

Asa closed the curtain over the window, blocking out the late evening sun. He left the room, and Deena followed behind.

"Mrs. Paty should be here soon to get you. Would you like to sit on the porch while we wait?"

"Sure."

Asa had no complaints about today. Mr. Thompson, the missionary, had said he could marry them at the end of next week. Alice was making a special gown for Deena for their wedding. They'd had a wonderful family supper. And now the day was ending with him sitting on the porch talking to Deena.

He could get used to this very easily.

Chapter Eleven

Deena walked next to Asa toward the front porch, stealing glances at the uninjured side of his face. Per usual, he made sure to walk on her left to hide his scars. From this angle, he looked much younger and daintier like Rob. She understood the desire to want to hide part of oneself from others.

Asa stopped in front of one of the two rocking chairs and waited for her to sit before doing the same. He descended into his chair with a gangly stiffness, and Deena patiently waited for him to get comfortable. He stretched out his leg and massaged up and down his thigh and calf.

His leg must be hurting real bad today because every time he tried to bend his knee, he winced, sucking in a sharp breath. Deena closed her eyes, rocking back and forth, giving him some semblance of privacy. The cool breeze on her face felt wonderful.

"It's beautiful, isn't it? Asa asked.

Deena looked at him. He lounged in his chair, the usual lines of strain around his eyes easing. Deena followed the direction of his gaze. Miles of green grass stretched into the horizon. A burst of yellow faded into a swathe of red that stretched into the blue of the evening sky.

"Yes. The sunset is quite stunning. It's so quiet and peaceful out here. I could get used to evenings like this."

Asa's chest rumbled with his laughter. "Good, because you will have to."

"You're right." Deena did her best to imitate his laughter, hoping he didn't notice the nervousness in it.

Thank goodness he didn't think much of her slip. She'd have to be more careful in the future.

They quieted, sitting next to each other, enjoying the scenery. She really could get used to nights like this. Family meals, easy conversation, and radiant sunsets.

Asa jerked. He reached down and held his leg, gritting his teeth, his face scrunched in pain. The strain eventually ebbed, then once again left him.

"I don't mean to pry, but would you mind telling me how you got injured?"

He was silent for a moment before continuing, "I fought for the Union in the war. There was a young man in my regiment named Joseph. He couldn't have been much past his seventeenth birthday, although he'd lied and said he'd turned twenty. He had no business fighting. He thought war was all about glory and honor. One day during a battle, I saw him curled up on the ground behind a tree, his hands on his head. He'd left his gun lying on the ground, leaving himself defenseless. A Reb saw him and started charging at him on his horse. I ran to him as fast as I could. I knocked Joseph out of the way before the Reb trampled him, but the horse collided with my side. Either slamming into the horse, or the fall, or both, busted up my leg and cut up my face."

"I'm sorry to hear that."

Asa waved off her sympathy. "It's all right. I'd do it again if I could. Joseph went home to his mother, unlike many young men. I'm happy to have played my part in making that happen."

"You're a brave man. Probably one of the finest I've ever met."

"That's high praise." Asa rubbed the back of his neck. "I'm just trying to spend my time living the best life I can. Some days are better than others, like everybody else's. I'm sure you've done your share of good deeds, as well."

It was Deena's turn to be abashed. "Some days, I don't know if I'll ever do enough good to outweigh all the bad that I've done."

Asa shook his head. He looked at her full-on for the first time, not caring about his scars. "It don't work like that." He covered her hand with his own, his expression gentle. "You can't earn your way into good graces. It's a gift. All the Lord wants is for you to turn to him and love him. He'll give you a clean start every day. No strings attached."

Deena sat silently, absorbing that revolutionary concept. It flew in the face of everything life had taught her. *Everyone* wanted something. No one ever gave you a clean start without expecting something in return. And the *clean* start they did give you still had a little dirt on it. Why would some all-powerful god be any different?

"Why?"

"Because he loves us. With a love that we can't understand."

"I agree with the not understanding part. I can't fathom how I'm supposed to forgive myself, let alone how He does."

He squeezed her hand, then let it go. "It gets easier with time."

Asa settled in his chair and continued to watch the sunset. She couldn't fully accept what he'd said, but she respected how he believed so strongly. Maybe one day she could too.

Off in the distance, a small dot on the horizon grew larger as someone approached. The wagon came closer until Deena spotted Mrs. Paty bobbing side to side in her seat.

She brought the horses to a stop in front of the house. "*Buena noches.*"

Asa stood and hobbled down the porch steps. "Good evening, Mrs. Paty. Thank you for coming to pick Deena up."

"My pleasure. Did you have a good day?

"Yes, ma'am. We got our wedding date set for next Thursday. We'll do it here at the house."

"Wonderful. I will fry up some chicken and whip up some mud apples. Let me know if you need anything else. I'll make sure all the ladies in town coordinate what they're going to bring."

"You don't have to do all that, Mrs. Paty," Deena said. The last thing she wanted was for this sham wedding to end up a large, public affair.

"Nonsense. This town loves Asa, and not a single person would think of missing his wedding. We're all more than happy to chip in."

Deena fisted and released the fabric of her skirt several times. There'd be yet another heap of embarrassment.

"I agree with Deena, but I know you won't take no for an answer, so I'll say thank you instead. You treat me too good, Mrs. Paty."

"There's no such thing. If you two don't mind, I'd like to get going. I'd like to be back home before the sun is completely gone."

"Of course not," Deena said. She climbed into the wagon, taking a seat next to Mrs. Paty.

"Good night, ladies. Stay safe."

"We will," Mrs. Paty replied. "Goodnight."

"Goodnight," Deena said to Asa.

Mrs. Paty snapped the reins, setting the horse off at a moderate pace. Deena waved at Asa, already doing something she hadn't in a long time.

Missing someone.

***

With the bucket of feed in her hand, Deena walked into the hencoop as she'd done every day for nearly a week. She hummed quietly to herself, enjoying the stillness of the early morning. It was so different out here. So much more peaceful than the crowded streets of New York City. The air smelled fresh and clean, not polluted with waste and disease.

The quiet lull of nature was much more delightful than shouting people, the grind of factory machines, and all the other city noises. If Deena had to define utopia, this would be it.

The back door of the house flew open, expelling a sprightly SaraGrace. The little girl ran towards her at full speed, the two braids Deena had put in her hair this morning flapping behind her.

SaraGrace bounded into the chicken pen, not stopping until she slammed into Deena's legs. She hugged them tightly, burying her face in Deena's skirt.

"Good morning, Mama."

She'd taken to calling Deena that ever since the night they'd prayed together. It still unnerved Deena every time SaraGrace did so, but she never corrected her. The poor child would be yet another casualty of the devastation left in the wake of her lie.

"Good morning, bug. Did you sleep well last night?"

"Yes, ma'am. Did you?"

"I sure did. Me and Mrs. Paty sat up talking for a little while before we went to bed."

"I wish I could have been there." SaraGrace poked out her bottom lip and crossed her arms. "I can't wait till you come and live with me and Papa. I'm so happy that I have a new mama. I don't remember my old one."

Deena's heart broke anew. Asa had done an amazing job raising his daughter so far, even without the presence of a mother. SaraGrace was full of life and love. Deena hoped she wouldn't be the cause of that falling to pieces when she left.

"Will you come play with me?" SaraGrace asked, her voice hopeful.

"I need to finish up my chores, but afterward, I will."

"I'll help you."

With the burst of energy that only young children possess, SaraGrace sprinted back into the house, reappearing a few minutes later with a small basket. She dipped into the hen house and collected the eggs while Deena finished feeding the chickens.

Taking care of the chickens was done faster with SaraGrace than Deena had ever done on her own. She might have to employ SaraGrace's help more often in the future. They walked back to the house to put the eggs away.

"What do we have to do next?" SaraGrace asked.

Deena bent down, so they were eye to eye, a genuine smile on her face. She had a feeling no matter how laborious the task, SaraGrace would be more than happy to help her complete it if it meant they'd be able to play once it was done.

"How about we..."

"If I can be rude enough to interrupt," Asa's smooth voice said, coming up behind them. "I thought we could take a break today." He looked at Deena. "This place will be partly yours soon. I can show you what you'll be getting. We can bring a picnic, too."

"I love picnics," SaraGrace exclaimed.

Deena nodded, absorbing some of SaraGrace's enthusiasm. "I'd like that."

"Good, because I already made one up. The buggy is ready, so let's go."

Deena untied her apron and tossed it onto the counter. One hand on her hip, she swept the other out in front of her. "Please lead the way, sir."

Asa extended his winged elbow, which Deena accepted. SaraGrace held her free hand, and together they left for their outing, feeling to Deena an awful lot like a family.

Chapter Twelve

"Look over there," Asa said, pointing to a herd of animals grazing in the distance.

"What are those, Papa?"

Deena squinted at the beasts. "They look like deer."

"Close. They're mule deer. See their big ears and the black fur on the tip of their tails? And watch this." Asa handed Deena the reins for a moment, then cupped his hands around his mouth and hollered as loud as he could.

The deer lifted their heads and turned, focusing on the small buggy and its occupants. SaraGrace mimicked her father and began yodeling through her cupped hands. The deer took off, bounding away with a stiff-legged gait that made them appear to be bouncing up and down.

Asa watched his girls, entranced by the delight and amusement alighting their faces. He took the reins back from Deena. She leaned forward, trying to get a better view of the spectacle nature performed solely for them. They watched until the deer became specks in the distance.

"That was amazing, Papa!" SaraGrace clapped her tiny hands as if she were in the audience of a grand opera giving a standing ovation.

Deena hugged SaraGrace closer to her side, laughing and grinning just as hard. "Yes, that was a moment I will never forget."

"I'm glad you both liked that. Being surrounded by nature is my favorite part of living out here. It makes me marvel at how it all works. How every single plant, animal, and insect has a role to play in the grand design of this wilderness."

"I like living out here too, Papa. Do you like living out here, Mama?"

Deena stroked SaraGrace's cheek, smiling down at the little girl. "I do." She gazed at Asa. "Your father is right. This place is magnificent in so many ways."

His eyes never leaving Deena's, Asa reached in the breast pocket on his vest and withdrew a hunk of wood. He kept it hidden, his fist blocking her view. "I hope you don't mind. I took the liberty of making you something. Just a small token of my appreciation for all that you've been doing."

"Aww, Asa. You didn't have to do that."

"I know. I wanted to. Hold out your hand."

He waited for Deena to do as he said. He touched his fist to her palm, then slowly opened his fingers, releasing the gift. A crackle of exhilaration shot up his arm, making him shudder at the contact. They looked at each other, their attention riveted. Did she feel it too?

Why would she? For a moment, Asa had forgotten himself. Forgotten what he looked like. He snatched back his hand, lest he did something else foolish, like try to hold hers.

Asa focused back on the landscape before them. "Carved it myself. I hope you like it."

Catching him off guard, Deena touched his scarred cheek, guiding his attention back to her and smiled. She glanced between the bear figurine and him. "It's perfect. Like the man who made it."

Roots sprouted from the seed of hope that had planted in his heart the day he'd picked her up from the train depot. As much as he tried to deny it, deep down Asa yearned for a woman to love him. Maybe he could have that with Deena.

He cleared his throat to remove the emotion clogging his voice. "Yes, well. I'm glad it pleases you."

"Thank you. No one has ever given me something so special. I will cherish it until the day I breathe my last breath."

Asa looked down and caught sight of SaraGrace sitting between them, her grin so broad that it pushed up her cheeks, making her eyes squint. Excitement, and an understanding beyond her years, shone in her perceptive blue eyes. She almost looked ready to spring out of her seat as high as the mule deer. It seemed he wasn't the only one with secret hopes and dreams about having a real family filled with love.

They traveled on a bit farther, talking and laughing as they went. Thankfully, Asa spotted his intended destination not much later.

"This looks like good as spot as any for our picnic." He parked the wagon next to a large white willow tree planted by a river.

"Is this part of your land as well?" Deena asked, amazement in her voice as she took in the scene before them.

"It is. We haven't left my plot yet."

Deena's mouth gaped. She surveyed their surroundings, nodding her head slowly. "I'm impressed. We've been riding for some time. I must admit you own a lot more than I realized. Not that it matters," she quickly amended. "I'm not here to take from you. I'm not after what you own."

"I'm not worried about that."

He wasn't. She'd barely allowed him to purchase a few dresses for her. And either way, once they married, he was more than happy to share all that he had with her. The entire point of him building this place up was for his family. The one she'd soon be his partner in creating.

"Papa, it's hot," SaraGrace whined. She threw a hand over her forehead and slumped to the side, emphasizing her distress. "Can we dip our feet in the water to cool off?"

Asa pressed his lips together to keep from laughing at her dramatic antics. Being a father came with some of the most entertaining moments of his life.

"Go right on ahead. I'll lay out the picnic."

"Yay! Thank you, Papa."

SaraGrace took Deena's hand and sprinted down to the riverbank. In short order, they removed their shoes and stockings, then waded into the water, hiking their skirts a little above their ankles. They frolicked at the edge of the shore, enjoying the coolness of the water on their bare skin.

SaraGrace kicked the water, spraying Deena, who laughed and splashed water back at her. A water fight soon ensued.

After laying out the blanket and food that he'd packed, Asa strolled down to the river. "Looks like you guys are having a lot of..." His face fell, his smile vanishing. "Get out. Get out of the water right now," he bellowed.

Deena and SaraGrace stood frozen for a moment, not understanding the sudden souring of his mood. He didn't have to repeat himself, though. Snapping into action, Deena grabbed SaraGrace's hand and hurried out of the water.

"Come on, bug. You heard your father."

Asa limped past them at a quick clip. Deena watched him go, holding SaraGrace securely to her side. He stopped and bent near the water not far from where they had been playing.

Deena's gasp carried to his ears a few seconds later. Her shock probably matched his ire. Asa stared down at two dead pigs with arrows sticking out of their sides. The carcasses were half in and half out of the water.

He glanced over his shoulder. Deena had turned SaraGrace's head away, pressing the side of her face into her stomach. He sent up a silent plea that his daughter hadn't seen the gruesome scene.

"Come on," Deena said, guiding SaraGrace away. "Let's clean up the picnic while your daddy handles his business."

"What's wrong? What happened?" SaraGrace asked.

"Don't worry about it right now. What we need to do is pick everything up and pack it away."

SaraGrace must have understood the unspoken censure in Deena's voice. She didn't ask any further questions. Satisfied that they would be all right, Asa focused back on the task at hand. He rolled his sleeves up to his elbows, then gripped the front hooves of one of the pigs and yanked it out of the water. His feet slipped several times on the soft mud along the shore, but eventually, he hauled the heavy corpse onto dry land. He went back in the water and did the same with the other dead animal.

It had been so peaceful for the past week that he'd almost forgotten the trouble they'd been having. Apparently, the trouble hadn't forgotten about him.

Asa trudged to the wagon, the front of his shirt and pants soaked. He raked a frustrated hand through his hair. "This river provides water for a lot of folks around here, especially for the townspeople. Those pigs could have contaminated the water. This is getting dangerous. We gotta get to the bottom of who is causing all this trouble."

Deena rubbed up and down his arm. "We'll figure this out together. I'll go digging for information tomorrow when I go into town to pick up my wedding dress from Alice."

"No. I don't want you to get yourself into any kind of trouble. I'll handle this."

"Wives help their husbands, and as your future wife, that's what I intended to do," Deena said, her voice full of resolution. She squared her shoulders, her gaze unwavering.

Pride welled in Asa's chest. She was a magnificent woman, and he was lucky to have her.

"I appreciate that, but the best way you can help is to stay safe. That way I can concentrate on what I need to do, knowing nothing bad will happen to you. And um..." Asa took hold of Deena's hand. "I think it would be best if we waited until all this is over before getting married. I don't want to leave you a widow right after we get hitched."

Deena winced as if his words physically pained her. Her voice dropped, losing some of its previous vigor. "I understand. That's probably for the best."

Did it make him an awful person, that the look of disappointment on her face lifted his mood? Could Deena's feelings for him be growing as his were for her? He hoped so.

"I'm sorry the picnic was ruined. We need to get back to the house," Asa said to both Deena and SaraGrace.

"I don't mind, Papa. I'm a big girl. I don't need picnics."

Asa smiled at his daughter. He could tell she was putting on a brave face for him. "Thank you both for being so understanding. Let's go."

He helped them back into the wagon, then climbed up in the seat and started them off back the way they'd come. He'd drop Deena off at Mrs. Paty's early today and then head over to Rob's to tell him what happened.

Chapter Thirteen

The irony of being a thief was that it tended to give a person a staunch case of paranoia. Making them terrified of becoming the victim. Deena clutched her reticule, both hands pressing it against her stomach.

A sheen of sweat coated her palms, but she dared not remove them from her plunder. The piece of paper she'd stolen from Bloodlow made the reticule feel like it weighed as much as a baby elephant. Or perhaps that was a delusion of her guilt and fear.

It had finally dawned on her last night to ask the missionary to read it. As a man of the cloth, honor and honesty was part of his moral creed. He wouldn't lie to her about what he read or, at the very least, he wouldn't steal it from her.

Once she knew for certain why the paper was so valuable to Bloodlow, she could figure out what she wanted to do with it. Either way, she had a feeling it would be her ticket out of the

Dakota Territory. Asa didn't want her help figuring out what was happening, and he'd postponed the wedding, making now the perfect time to leave.

Deena breathed a little easier when she stepped into Alice's dress shop. She trusted the woman implicitly. As she'd said the first time that she'd come into the shop, she really could see them being good friends. The only reason she hadn't asked Alice to read the letter was because she couldn't be sure if her loyalties lay with Asa. And Alice might start asking questions about why Deena had the paper in the first place, or about other things she didn't want to answer.

"Afternoon, Deena." Alice greeted her as soon as she walked through the door.

"Hey, Alice. I have some news for you. Oh… I'm sorry. I didn't mean to intrude."

A man stood on the platform in front of the mirror, his arms out while Alice stuck a few pins in the coat he wore. Deena's guard immediately rose again.

"You're not intruding. Let me introduce you to Mr. Baile. He owns the livery on the other side of town."

"*Enchanté, mademoiselle.* It is a pleasure," the man said, awkwardly bowing at the waist to avoid being stabbed by the many sharp pins sticking out everywhere.

"Same." Deena turned to Alice. "I can come back later if you'd like."

"Nonsense," Mr. Baile answered. "We are almost finished here. And I am the one who is the intruder. This is a dress shop meant for the creation of apparel for the fairer sex. I just love Alice's work. Jude does a wonderful job at his tailor shop, but Alice has a true gift. Her work is unparalleled. I trust no one else with my wardrobe."

"You flatter me, Mr. Baile."

"No flattery at all. Only the simple truth. Anyhow, Miss Deena, I do believe congratulations are in order. It is a pleasure to meet the woman who has captured the heart of Asa Grantt. I can say with complete confidence that he is one of the best men these parts have to offer."

"I don't know if I would say I've captured his heart. But I'm glad to be marrying him."

Deena didn't have to lie when she said that. If life had given her a different destiny and she could truly marry Asa, she'd be a very happy woman.

"Balderdash! Since you arrived, that man has smiled more than I've ever seen him do and relinquished his growly personality."

"I agree," Alice chimed in from beneath Mr. Baile's armpit.

"That's a nice piece of jewelry," Deena said, both changing the subject and admiring his beaded necklace. Five strings of beads hung from his neck, the length of each layer increasing. Leather strips draped on either side of the bone-white beads with what appeared to be animal claws dangling from their tips.

"Thank you. It was a gift from Chief Struck by the Ree during my last visit to the reservation."

"You've been to the reservation?" Deena came closer to the platform. "How long ago?"

"Yes. Due to recent events taking place on everyone's farms, I asked the chief for permission to visit and discuss what was happening."

Deena waited, but Mr. Baile didn't say anything else. He looked at himself in the mirror, his expression nonchalant, as if it were the most natural thing in the world to leave a conversation unfinished. The impish gleam in his eyes gave Deena the sneaking suspicion he was enjoying being the only person apprised of such important information.

"What did the two of you talk about?" she finally asked.

"A great many things. The most important is that his people are not responsible for the attacks happening in Ruby Creek. They are simply trying to live and adjust to life on the reservation. They want no trouble from us. The Ihanktonwan people have suffered greatly in the last several years. All they want is to coexist peacefully."

Alice stepped back, finished with her work. Hands on her hips, she waited for him to take off the coat and asked, "And you believe Chief Struck by the Ree?"

"Without a doubt. He is a man of honor, even though many have not given him the same courtesy." He focused on Deena. "I heard about the incident with the pigs in the river yesterday. I can assure you the Ihanktonwan people had nothing to do with it."

Deena nodded in agreement. "For what it's worth, I believe you. The first night I was here, I saw a feather headdress that the real culprits left on Alice and Jonathan's farm. I don't know much about their culture, but I knew enough to tell that someone was trying to frame the Ihanktonwan."

"It's nice to know I have an ally. I understand their concern, but I fear people are letting go of reason in exchange for an easy enemy to blame." He shook his head. "However, that solves nothing in the end."

"Agreed," Deena replied.

"I, for one, want the real bandits caught and tried for this whole thing," Alice added. "That way, we can get on with our lives and not have to sleep with one eye open all the time. We worked hard proving up our land and making this town something we can be proud of. No sneaky rascal is going to take that away from us."

Mr. Baile stared off at nothing in particular, slowly stroking his chin. "I have my suspicions about who the real culprits are, but I won't share them until I have more proof."

"If you need help in any way, let us know," Alice said.

"Yes, please do," Deena agreed.

"Thank you, ladies, for that generous offer. I hope never to have to take you up on it, as I'd hate to put you in harm's way, but I shall if I must." He handed his coat to Alice, then picked up his hat. "Now, if you will excuse me, I must be going. It was lovely chatting with you both."

"Come back by next Tuesday, and I'll have this ready for you."

"Thank you. Farewell."

Mr. Baile exited the shop with all the pomp and prance of an English dandy. Deena giggled to herself. She liked him.

Alice draped his coat across a nearby table, then turned back to Deena. "You mentioned having news for me. Tell me while I grab your wedding dress. We should only have to do this one fitting, then I can finish it up."

"That's what I came to talk to you about, actually. You don't have to rush on my dress. Asa and I aren't getting married on Thursday."

Alice whirled around, her eyes wide and glossy as porcelain teacups. She grabbed Deena's arms, holding her at arm's length as if she didn't know whether to hug or shake her. "What do you mean, you aren't getting married? What happened?"

Deena held up her hands in surrender. "No, nothing bad happened. Asa decided he didn't want to marry until all this is over. He's trying to keep me safe."

"Oh, good. Next time start with that." Alice placed a hand on her chest. "You scared me.

Had my heart about ready to burst. After what Billie put Asa through, I can't stand seeing that poor man getting hurt again. That harlot nearly broke him. If it weren't for SaraGrace, he might have lost himself at the bottom of a bottle."

The ever-present dull ache of guilt flared up inside Deena. She almost wanted to tell Alice not to be relieved just yet. "What happened between them?"

"Not my story to tell. But I'm sure if you ask him, Asa will share the details with you."

"You're right. I should hear it from him."

"Well, shoot. I had my mouth fixed on eating some of Mrs. Paty's mud apples. I don't know how she makes them taste so good."

"Sorry to ruin your chance of having some of Mrs. Paty's cooking. I feel the pain of that loss, too."

Alice scratched her hairline near her temple. Then, she slapped her thigh, her face lighting up with an idea. "You know what. Everyone was planning on making stuff anyway. We can throw a barn dance instead. We'll push it back to Saturday to give us time to prepare."

"That sounds like a good time."

"Hopefully, it will lift everyone's spirits. We're overdue for some fun around here. I'll coordinate with Mrs. Paty." Alice tapped the platform with the toe of her shoe. "Well, get on up here and let's still do this fitting. I won't rush, but I'll still work on it, so it'll be ready whenever you need it."

Alice walked away to retrieve the dress, and Deena stepped up onto the platform. She kept her gaze on the ground, unable to look at herself in the mirror. She didn't want to see herself in the wedding dress. The symbol of the life she desperately wanted, but wasn't going to have. This was all temporary. Sooner or later the real Pearl would show up to claim what was rightfully hers.

Chapter Fourteen

Deena stood outside the small, one-room church, unable to make herself enter. The large, black cross affixed above the door contrasted with the rest of the white exterior, making it shine like a beacon of hope to some, and a warning to those like her.

Maybe she shouldn't go in. After all, she planned to ask a man of God to help her decipher something she'd stolen from someone else. There had to be some sacred biblical law she was breaking by roping the missionary into her sin. Resolve shaken, Deena turned to leave.

"May I help you?"

Deena spun back around. A gentleman wearing a black frock coat over a black waistcoat and a crisp, well-pressed white shirt, stood in the previously empty doorway of the church.

He appeared to be in his mid-to-late fifties. His long, bushy sideburns—the only hair on his otherwise clean-shaven face—grazed the top of his stiff lifted collar. The black stock tie cinched close to his neck almost appeared to be choking him.

"May I help you?" he repeated.

Deena took an unconscious step back. Her irrational fear must be reaching new heights. It was making her imagine his voice had an oily, fiendish quality to it.

"Good day, sir. My name is Deena Lyon. Are you the missionary here assigned to this church?"

"Indeed, I am. My name is Mr. Luke Thompson. Reverend Stevens is traveling around the state to other churches, so I am here in his stead. You're the woman I was supposed to marry to Asa Grantt, aren't you?"

"Yes. That's me. I'm in need of your assistance if you have a moment to spare."

"I always have time for anyone in need. Please come in." He stepped to the side and held an arm out, beckoning her to come inside.

If he meant for the twisted curl of his lips to be a reassuring smile, he failed miserably. The prickling sensation in Deena's scalp turned into a full shiver. He reminded her of the serpent tempting Adam and Eve into losing their home in the Garden of Eden.

Stop spinning such tall tales. He's not out to get you.

Deena licked her lips and walked up to the church door. She hesitated for a moment before stepping over the threshold.

The inside was simply decorated. Several more crosses hung on the spaces between the three large windows on the right and left sides of the building. Eight rows of wooden benches lined each side, leaving a wide aisle in the middle.

A map lay on one of the benches, next to a notebook and pencil. She recognized the name Ruby Creek printed across the top. She'd made sure to memorize the written form of the town name before coming here just in case. Three more words she couldn't read were printed in the bottom right corner. Something told her to remember what those words looked like.

"How may I help you today?" Mr. Thompson asked, closing the door behind them.

Deena wanted to demand he open it back. To give her a clear escape and increase the chance that someone would hear her if she screamed.

"I must confess that before coming to Ruby Creek, I stole something from a man, and since being here, I've been feeling guilty about it." She reached into her reticule and withdrew the paper she'd stolen from Bloodlow. "I want to return it to the man, but I'm not sure what it is. It's probably worthless, and returning it isn't a valuable use of my time, but I want to make sure before I dismiss the notion. I never learned to read. I can only recognize a few words here and there, so I was hoping you could do so for me. To help me decide what to do next."

She held out the paper. Before Mr. Thompson's fingers even touched it, his eyes went owlish, and he sucked in a sharp inhale. His upright, virtuous facade fell away, revealing the greedy swindler beneath.

"I'll be." He tore his eyes away from the paper and looked at Deena. "You said you don't know what this is?"

Instinct told her to amend her declaration about her illiteracy, but the damage had already been done. "That is correct."

This was a bad idea. She shouldn't have come to him for help. If anything, she should have risked asking Alice. Nothing about this man sat well with her.

"I'm glad you came to me. This is a bounty."

"A bounty?" Deena repeated.

"Yes. On a rather notorious outlaw. Hence the reward being so high."

That made no sense. Why would Bloodlow be carrying around a copy of his own bounty? "What about this picture here of the eagle? Why is that on there? Don't bounties have pictures of the outlaw's face on them?"

Mr. Thompson shrugged. "Some do. Some don't. It all depends on if the lawmen had a good description of the man or not. And this is a federal bounty, hence the eagle."

He was lying. Deena could sense it in the pit of her stomach. But she didn't know enough about the topic to say for sure.

"You should leave this here with me. I'll make sure to get it to the authorities."

"Thank you, but no. I will handle it myself."

Deena gripped the paper and tugged. Mr. Thompson didn't let it go at first.

"Are you sure?" he asked, reluctantly releasing it. "I can take care of that easy. You wouldn't have to bother yourself with going down to the sheriff's musty, old office."

"That's quite all right. I don't mind. Won't be a bother at all."

"Where did you say you got that from?"

"I lifted it from a man named Pete Bloodlow."

The color drained from Mr. Thompson's face. He pulled on the collar of his shirt as if he were suddenly having trouble breathing. Bloodlow's reputation must have spread farther than Deena realized.

"Well, if you will excuse me, I must be going."

"May God bless you," he replied, the first ounces of sincerity entering his voice since their conversation began.

Deena spun on her heels and headed out the door. Mr. Thompson didn't attempt to stop her. He watched her leave, a sadness in his expression as if he were watching someone march to their death.

This trip had been a waste of time. She still didn't know what the paper said, and now had a feeling something terrible was coming her way.

Home. She wanted to go home. To Asa. The only place that had made her feel safe in a very long time.

Chapter Fifteen

A sprinkle of cinnamon, nutmeg, and sugar over each layer. That was the secret to making the best sweet potato pie, according to Mrs. Paty. Miss a layer or forget one of those ingredients, and the taste wouldn't be the same.

Deena repeated the combination over and over, trying not to forget it. She'd gotten it in her head to bake a pie for Asa as a "thank you, I'm sorry, and thinking about you" gift. Although she'd keep that last part to herself when she presented it to him. If she ever presented it to him. Baking required patience and other skills she was learning she didn't possess.

"Knead the dough, *querida*. Not beat it." Mrs. Paty said, coming through the back door into the kitchen.

She placed the basket of laundry she'd just taken down from the line on a counter and came up beside Deena. Mrs. Paty *tsked* at her rather harsh technique of handling the dough.

"Sorry." Deena eased the amount of force she used on the gooey lump of flour.

"When a woman handles her baking like that, she's either angry, hungry, or both. Which is it for you?" Mrs. Paty grinned.

Deena stopped kneading. She leaned both hands on the counter and hung her head. "Scared. I'm really scared."

"Scared?" Mrs. Paty's eyebrows knitted together. She hugged Deena tight. "Oh *mija*, what's wrong? Tell me how I can help fix it."

Deena rested her chin on Mrs. Paty's shoulder, inhaling her soothing lavender scent. When she pulled away, Mrs. Paty gripped both of her flour-covered hands, refusing to break their connection. Deena didn't mind. She needed it. The strength of someone else nearby, standing with her in the midst of her troubles. She was tired of being alone.

Now she was hopeful she didn't have to be.

"I made a mistake. A big one. Several, in fact." She scoffed at the understatement of her stupidity. "And now I don't know how to fix any of it without hurting Asa."

"Sometimes the truth hurts, but that doesn't excuse us from telling it. You've made mistakes." Mrs. Paty shrugged a shoulder. "We all have. Now you have the chance to learn and grow from it. To be a stronger woman."

Deena shook her head. "I don't know if I can."

"You can, *mija*. Nothing you've done is so big that it can't be forgiven."

"I'm not Pearl Wilson," Deena blurted out. "My name is Deena Lyon. I was in a restaurant when I overheard Pearl speaking with Mrs. Crenshaw about Asa and how she couldn't move out here and marry him for two months. So, I stole some of her letters and decided to take her place. Temporarily, until I could figure out what I wanted to do next."

Mrs. Paty touched her fingers to the base of her throat. She stared through Deena. "Oh, dear. That is *una muy grande* lie. Come, let's sit."

They walked over to the dining table and sat across from each other. Once they were seated, Mrs. Paty immediately took hold of Deena's hands again. One day Deena hoped to be able to express how much that small gesture meant to her.

"Why did you do it?"

"Because of this." Deena reached in her skirt pocket and extracted the piece of paper that had started it all. She pushed it across the table to Mrs. Paty. "I stole it from a criminal named Pete

Bloodlow. He hunted me down and caught me afterward, demanding I give it back. I'd probably be dead if a group of strangers hadn't helped me."

Mrs. Paty examined the paper. Unlike Mr. Thompson, her eyes didn't glaze over with greed. Instead, she looked good and terrified.

"Do you know what this is?"

"No. I can't read."

"Can't read? But you took Pearl's letters."

"I only know a few words that I've memorized. Basic words to help me get around and survive. But not enough to read full sentences or a book."

"Then how… Wait." Mrs. Paty took a calming breath. "Tell me your story. Start from the beginning, please."

"Not much of a story to tell." Deena extracted her hands from Mrs. Paty's and wrapped them around her middle. "I ran away from my plantation in Virginia after my sixteenth birthday and headed up north. My old master's son Mark started taking liberties I never agreed to give. I ended up in New York City. No one would give me a job, not even the factories.

I was another dirty ragamuffin from the South who couldn't read or write in a horde of people just like me, all wanting the same thing.

So, I started stealing to survive. I got real good at it. I watched high-class women and mimicked how they dressed and talked. That helped me blend in, so no one got suspicious when I came around to rob them. Then, I stole from the wrong man and had to run away again to save my life. I saw Pearl show Mrs. Crenshaw the letters Asa had written to her. I stole them and paid someone to read them to me. That's how I ended up here."

Mrs. Paty rose from her chair and paced back and forth. "This is a bearer bond." She held up the paper. "Do you know what that is?"

Deena shook her head. "No."

"This piece of paper gives the person who holds it the right to claim the amount written on the front."

"So, I can turn that in for money?"

"Yes. Five thousand dollars, to be exact."

Deena leaped from her chair, knocking it over, and stumbled backward. "Five thousand dollars!"

No wonder Bloodlow had hunted her down. That was more money than she ever hoped to see in her life. And the missionary had lied to her. But why hadn't he stolen it from her?

Because she'd said Bloodlow's name. Clearly, Mr. Thompson recognized who he was. He probably knew as well as she did, there was no way Bloodlow would let someone get away with stealing that much money from him.

"I need to leave. I have to get out of here. Asa and SaraGrace aren't safe with me here. Bloodlow is going to keep hunting me down until he gets this back."

"No!" Mrs. Paty rushed over to Deena and grabbed her by the arms. "You will tell Asa the truth."

"What? No, I can't. I need to leave."

"You care for Asa, don't you?"

"Yes, I do, which is why I need to run. I have to protect him from the mess I've created."

Mrs. Paty gently cupped Deena's cheek. "You ran from Virginia, then ran from New York. It never brought you peace. Stop running, *mija*. Tell Asa everything. He cares for you too. I can see it in the way he looks at you. Let him help you. The two of you can figure out how to handle this situation together."

"But he already has so much to deal with. I don't want to burden him further."

"Helping the ones we love is never a burden. It is a sacrifice, yes, but never a burden. I wish my George were still alive. I'd do anything he asked of me, no matter how big or small."

Deena bit the inside of her cheek. She suddenly desperately needed a drink of water to quench her parched throat. Telling Asa was the right thing to do. She couldn't deny that. What she couldn't believe was that telling him the truth wouldn't lead to him seeing her differently. Right now, she was someone he was willing to spend the rest of his life with. Someone he looked out for and protected. If she told him she was a liar and a thief, he wouldn't want her anymore.

Call her a fool, but Deena didn't want to be around when he no longer looked at her with admiration and trust. When his words turned bitter and mean. She wanted her memories of their time together to remain unstained by the damage of the hurt and betrayal she'd inflicted.

But that was selfish.

"You're right, Mrs. Paty. I need to tell Asa the truth. I *will* tell Asa the truth."

"I know you will. You are a good woman, Deena. You won't be able to help doing the right thing in the end."

"Thank you for saying that."

"I'm only speaking the truth. Now, come on." Mrs. Paty strolled back to the counter with the forgotten lump of dough. "Let's finish that pie. Maybe you can use it to get on his good side before you tell him."

Deena could only hope. At this point, she'd use any trick she could to keep Asa from hating her. If only it truly were as easy as baking him a pie.

Chapter Sixteen

Wagon wheels rolled over the hard, compact dirt leading up to his home, capturing Asa's attention. His cupped hands stopped halfway to his face. Water dripped between his fingers back into the washbasin.

Deena was here.

The heaviness that had been pressing on his chest all yesterday finally lifted. He'd only been without her for one day, and his body thrummed with the need to be near her again.

Asa made quick work of the rest of his morning routine. He dunked a cloth in the chilly water and scrubbed his face and neck with hurried strokes. His tooth powder was in his mouth, then rinsed out, faster than ever before. He pulled the straps of his suspenders over his shoulders as he walked out of his bedroom.

"Mornin', ladies." He greeted Mrs. Paty and Deena on the porch, his eyes never left the latter.

She'd braided her hair into two long plaits along her scalp that ran from the top of her head down the base of her head. The ends hung over her shoulders. He should tell her how much he liked it. SaraGrace would no doubt want her hair done in the same way once she saw it.

"Good morning, *mijo*."

"Morning, Asa."

Although she spoke to him, Deena kept her gaze averted. She stood a little behind Mrs. Paty as if using her as a protective shield. Some of the tightness returned to Asa's chest. Was something wrong? Was she upset with him? Did something happen yesterday?

"I'm sure you already have but did you two eat already?" he asked, trying to keep the disappointment from his voice. "I was just about to whip up some eggs and bacon for SaraGrace and me."

"Thank you, but yes, I've already eaten," Mrs. Paty answered.

"I can put on some coffee if you like."

"No, no. I need to get going. I'm going to visit Beatrice today. Her daughter Jane just had another baby, so she is excited to be able to babble about being a grandmother again."

"Tell her I said congratulations."

"Will do."

"Oh, and SaraGrace and I will bring Deena back tonight."

"Sounds good. You two have a good day."

Mrs. Paty looked pointedly at Deena before climbing back into the seat of her buckboard and heading off. Deena's chin dipped, understanding—and he assumed not liking—the unspoken message in that look. What was going on? She'd barely spoken a full sentence to him.

"Here." Deena held out a pie, still not meeting his eyes. "I made this for you last night. Mrs. Paty helped."

The sweet confection smelled wonderful. Sweet potato pie, he'd guess. If he weren't so worried about something being the matter with her, his mouth would probably be watering, ready to take a bite. He took the offered pie but paid it no mind.

"Is everything all right? You seem upset." He'd never been one to mince words, and he needed to know what was happening with her so he could fix it.

"Asa, I… You see…" Deena wrung her hands. She opened her mouth but didn't speak. Finally, she said, "May I ask what happened between you and your first wife? Billie."

Asa's lips curled into a slow smile. He wiped a hand over his face, expelling a relieved breath.

"That's it? Is that what's bothering you?" He laughed. "I'm more than happy to tell you about my marriage to Billie. Never be afraid to ask me anything. I will always be honest with you."

"Yeah, that's it. That's what's bothering me."

If it were possible to combust from elation, Asa would have done so. The urge to do a jig swept over him, but he refrained. Deena had no reason to feel insecure about his relationship with Billie, and he'd make sure she fully understood that.

"Me and Billie were born and raised in Chagrin Falls, Ohio. We lived not too far from each other, and our mamas were friends. They made up their minds that we were going to get married before we were out of the cradle. I didn't complain much about it. Billie was a beautiful girl and real sweet. We played together all the time, so we knew everything about each other. We got married when I was twenty and she was eighteen, right before I shipped out to go fight in the war. When I came back all broken and scarred, things weren't the same between us. I could tell she no longer liked the way I looked."

Deena touched his forearm, shaking her head. "No, Asa, don't say that. That can't be true."

"It was. Towards the end, she told me as much."

"I'm sorry."

"I couldn't change what'd been done, so I tried my best to make her happy in other ways. Taking good care of her. Making sure she had everything she needed. Then, I got the notion to follow Paul out here. At first, Billie was excited. She was nicer, and I saw more of the woman I'd known before the war. But once we got here and started working the land, she began getting cranky and bitter again, then downright mean.

I won't go too deep into it because I'm not trying to bad mouth her, but things got tough between us. I thought having a baby would soften her up, but she didn't like being around SaraGrace. One day I came home and found a note saying that she'd been writing letters to some rich fella in Boston, and he'd paid for her to passage there. Said she was divorcing me and once it was done to never contact her again about anything. Including SaraGrace."

"Asa, I…"

"Nothing to be said." He shifted the pie from one hand to the other, then scratched the back of his neck. He didn't want her to feel bad for him. "Billie hurt me bad, can't lie about that. But I will never hold you accountable for her mistakes. What me and you have is based upon how we treat each other. I'll never lie to you, and I hope you'll never lie to me."

Deena's hand fell away from his arm. She bunched her skirt in her hands and stared at the ground. "What if I did? Lie. Would that change the way you see me?"

He thought about that for a moment. Everyone made mistakes, and he'd show her grace for hers. At the same time, his heart couldn't take much more of a bruising from a woman he cared about.

"I guess that depends on what you lied about. Did you lie about something?"

"No," she blurted.

"Good." Hard conversation over, Asa led Deena into the house. "So now that we got that out of the way, I was thinking about taking you and SaraGrace into town to the ice cream soda fountain at Shumaker & Brown's Drug Store. We could go after we get finished working today."

"Are you sure? Harvest time is coming up soon. Shouldn't you be focusing on that?" She took the pie from him and placed it on the dining table.

"SaraGrace'll love the treat. And don't worry, Johnny is managing most of that." Asa patted his leg. "This isn't making it easy for me to work as much. We're working on hiring a few more men to help out for the season. Plus, I believe that after God, my family is the most important thing in my life. Taking care of you means spending time with you, as much as it does feeding you."

Deena smiled, that genuine breath-stealing smile he loved. "How can I refuse when you say it like that?"

"You can't. I won't let you." He winked at her. "SaraGrace is in her room. I'll be out in the fields if you need me. I'll try to be done around noon."

"See you... Oh, wait. When I told Alice about us postponing the wedding, she suggested having a barn dance next week instead. Said it would give people a chance to have some fun."

"We could use a good time around here. I warn you, though, I can't dance. I can never catch the rhythm of the music."

Deena laughed. He could almost see the picture she was conjuring in her mind of him fumbling around the dance floor. "Don't worry, I'm an excellent dancer. I'll help you."

"Some people can't be helped."

"Nonsense. We'll have a great time."

Asa shook his head. "I tried to warn you."

"I'm not afraid of a challenge. Now go on, get out of here. I suddenly have a hankering for ice cream soda water, and you're keeping me from it."

"Yes, ma'am." Asa grabbed his hat from the hook by the door, then headed out, an upbeat whistle on his lips and a lightness in his step.

***

Deena swept the dust from the front porch, doing her best to tidy up the house and keep herself busy until Asa came back to get them. She was looking forward to going to the soda fountain with him and SaraGrace. She'd never been to one before, even though there were plenty to chose from in New York. Living in the bowels of poverty didn't afford her such luxuries.

"Ready to go?" Asa asked, coming around the side of the house.

She'd been ready since he announced the plan to go this morning. Deena faced him, fixing her lips to tell him exactly that when she fully took him in. The strain around his eyes and mouth was too prominent to ignore. He nearly dragged his bad leg behind him. Deena's excitement quickly gave way to concern.

"You're in pain," she stated.

"Nothing too bad," Asa replied.

He was lying. A blind man could see the blaring signs of his discomfort. Deena propped the broom against the side of the house, then walked up beside Asa.

"Put your arm over my shoulder," she commanded, in a voice that brokered no arguments.

"I'm fine. I don't…"

"Put your arm over my shoulder," she repeated.

Asa did as she said. He leaned a little on Deena, although he held back from putting his full weight on her. She wrapped an arm around his waist, to better anchor him to her and offer support. They trudged up the porch with slow, even steps.

Deena deposited him in his rocking chair, then ran inside the house. She came back out a short time later with an empty bucket, a bowl of water, and a small rag. She flipped the bucket upside down and scooted it next to his foot.

"Lift your leg."

She helped Asa as he struggled to comply with her instructions. Together they got his leg elevated on top of the bucket. Deena hiked his pant leg up then dipped the rag in the cool water and placed it on his red and swollen knee. Asa sighed in relief.

"Thank you. I should be ready to go shortly."

Deena gently pressed the damp cloth, massaging his leg as best she could. "No. We aren't going anywhere today."

"But…"

"But nothing. The soda fountain isn't going anywhere. You need to rest. You've done such a great job taking care of me, now it's my turn to take care of you."

Asa relaxed into his chair. Deena could feel his eyes on her, although she kept her focus on the task in front of her.

"This is strange for me," he confessed.

"What?"

"Having someone else take care of me."

"Yeah well, get used to it," Deena said with a harrumph.

You can't make those kinds of promises. Maybe not for the long term, but for the rest of the time she was here, Deena would no longer let Asa ignore his own needs to put on a brave face for others. She'd make sure he started taking better care of himself. It was the least she could do to repay his kindness.

And more importantly, to show him without words how much he meant to her. Asa was a remarkable man and she'd miss him when she left.

He placed his hand over hers. "Thank you."

Deena nodded. Emotion clogged her throat. Helping him felt good. It felt right. So much so she wished it would never end. But eventually it would. She sat next his chair wishing the days would move slower. If only.

Chapter Seventeen

Asa hadn't been lying when he said he couldn't dance. Deena bit her bottom lip to keep from laughing at his gangly, uncoordinated movements. He tapped his heel when he should have tapped his toes. When everyone else spun to the left, he spun to the right. She tried, again and again, to teach him—even going so far as to move his feet for him—but she might as well have been talking gibberish. They'd moved to the edge of the dancing area, so his lack of skill wouldn't disrupt everyone else.

"No, no, no. *Three* steps forward, then bow," she instructed him.

He looked down at his feet. "Isn't that what I'm doing?"

"You're taking four steps."

"Watch me do it, Papa," SaraGrace said.

She executed the steps perfectly, then stepped back, hands on her hips, waiting for her father to repeat what she'd done. Asa tried again, and again, and again, getting worse with each attempt.

"How about we move on to something else?" he said. "Let's try what they're doing."

Deena followed the direction he pointed to the nearest couple moving in sync with the quick tempo set by the fiddler. The partners grabbed each other's left hands, pulled away, walked halfway around, let go, then stepped forward.

She nearly doubled over laughing. "If you can't get three steps and a bow, you won't get that."

"Yeah, Papa, that's hard even for me," SaraGrace said, her expression doubtful. "I don't think you can do that."

"I'm feeling up for an adventure." He moved his feet in a wild, made-up jig, ending it with a heel tap.

Deena stepped back. "My toes are not."

"You wound me, madam." He spread his fingers against his chest; his elbow lifted high in an exaggerated show of outrage. "I will go find someone who doesn't mind my peculiar style of movement."

"I believe you will find Rob over there."

Deena laughed with Asa so hard her stomach and cheeks began to ache. She hadn't laughed so much since her youth. These would be the happy memories that sustained her in the hard times throughout the rest of her life.

"It's for the best," Asa said, bending over. "My leg isn't feeling that great right now. Please continue without me."

SaraGrace grabbed Deena's hand and dragged her back into the cluster of the other dancers. "Come on, Mama. Now we can really dance."

They joined everyone else, stepping forward and then back, putting their hands in the middle and spinning in a circle, then turning around and spinning in the opposite direction. Deena couldn't keep her gaze from occasionally wandering over to Asa.

She watched him standing next to the table laden with pies, cookies, and other baked goods and sweet treats, talking to Rob and some of the other men. He was handsome under normal circumstances, but right now, laughing and being carefree, he was alluring in a new way. He made her want to be near him, soaking in the effervescent joy rolling off of him.

"Howdy, Deena," Alice said, catching her off guard. She waved from a little way away on the edge of the dance floor.

Deena jumped, quickly averting her unblinking stare from Asa. She walked over to her friend, leaving SaraGrace to continue twirling with a group of other children. "Hey, Alice."

"Don't stop looking at him on my account," she teased.

Deena's face flamed. "What can I say? I like the way he looks when he looks the way he does now. Well, I like the way he looks at the time, but especially when he looks so happy."

She and Alice giggled, sharing a knowing glance.

"I'm glad he has you. Listen," Alice sobered. "She didn't tell me exactly what you lied about, but Mrs. Paty said you have been keeping something from Asa. She wanted me to try to convince you to tell him."

"I want to. I do, but…"

"You're scared of losing him."

Deena nodded her head. "I've been trying to tell him all week. Every time I do, he does something wonderful, and I don't want to ruin things between us."

"Come with me."

Deena followed Alice out of the barn into the warm night. Stars glittered above them, igniting the darkness.

When they were far enough away from the barn not to be heard, Alice took Deena's hands in hers. "We haven't known each other for that long, but I can tell you're exactly what Asa needs, and he's exactly what you need. You owe it to Asa and yourself to clear things up between you two."

"What do I do if he doesn't want me anymore once I tell him?"

"That won't…"

"If it does. What do I do?"

"You move on, knowing that the Lord has something else in store for you."

Deena didn't want something else. She wanted *this* life. She wanted Asa to be her husband and SaraGrace to be her daughter. She wanted to expand their family and stay by his side until the day they both died. But she couldn't take that choice from Asa. If he chose her thinking that she was someone else, he wasn't really choosing her.

"Will you come with me? Be nearby in case I need support?"

"Yes. I'll be right…"

A loud war cry split the air, interrupting their conversation. Deena whipped around, searching pitch blackness for the source of the disturbance. The darkness was so thick, she couldn't see anything.

The call came again this time, accompanied by several other equally loud, screeching voices. Pounding drums joined the noise, adding to the confusion. Men and women poked their heads out of the barn, to figure out what was happening.

Whoever was behind this purposely tried to make it sound as if they were a band of Ihanktonwan warriors on the verge of attacking this gathering of innocent people.

This wasn't them. Deena believed Mr. Baile's assurance that they weren't the cause of the destruction happening around Ruby Creek.

"We have to go," Deena said, dragging Alice back toward the barn.

"What's happening?"

"I think we're being attacked."

Proving Deena's assumption, a shot rang out, whizzing through the air and hitting the wall of the barn with a thunk. Panic broke out. People ducked low, screaming and running around the structure, seeking shelter. More shots rang out, hitting the barn and the ground, adding to the deafening noise of terrified shrieks and fake Indian war cries.

Something flew by Deena's head. It struck the barn, along with the bullets. As they neared the barn, she could see the object more clearly.

An arrow. Several stuck out from the wooden structure.

Deena and Alice made it back into the barn unscathed. People ran in every direction. Some were leaving through the door they'd just entered. Others were climbing up to the haylofts.

"I need to find Jonathan," Alice said, tearing her hand from Deena's.

The selfish fear of being alone made Deena want to call out to her friend and beg her not to leave. It was too late. Alice had already disappeared into the crowd of frantic people.

Deena pulled rasping breaths into her lungs, trying to keep herself from dropping to the ground and curling up into a ball of panic. She couldn't afford the luxury of giving in. She had her own family to find, Asa and SaraGrace. She needed to find them and make sure they were safe.

She cupped her hands around her mouth and shouted, "Asa! SaraGrace! Where are you?"

"Deena, Deena," Asa called back.

"Mama!" SaraGrace whimpered.

They must be together. Good. She craned her neck, searching the area for them. The number of people in the barn had thinned, making it a little easier, but not much. The remaining individuals moved too much for her to see clearly.

"Asa, I can't see you," she shouted, moving in the direction she thought she heard his voice coming from. "Asa."

Two large, calloused hands grabbed Deena's arms. She struggled against the hold.

"Easy, easy. It's me," Asa's rich baritone voice crooned next to her ear. "I got you. You're safe."

Deena spun around and flung her arms around Asa's neck. She hugged him so tight she might've done him bodily harm if he weren't such a huge man. He hugged her back, rocking them side to side.

SaraGrace's small arms encircled her legs, holding on tight and pressing her body closer. She buried her face in Deena's skirt. Deena held onto SaraGrace, needing the comfort of touching her and feeling the movement of her body with each breath she took.

"We need to get out of here," Asa said, pulling away from their embrace.

He picked up SaraGrace and placed her in Deena's arms. Deena held onto her, curling her body around the little girl to shield her from any flying ammunition. Before she could start running, Asa swept Deena into his arms and held her close.

He did his best to use his body to shield them both. He moved slowly, straining under the collective weight of carrying them. A tremor started in his leg and ricocheted throughout his entire body.

"Put me down. I can walk."

"No," he said, his teeth clenched, and the skin around his eyes bunching in a pained grimace.

Deena wanted to argue. He'd complained about his leg bothering him not long ago, and clearly, the strain of carrying her and SaraGrace was too much. He was going to hurt himself if he kept this up. But opposing him would do no good.

Asa was a protector. He'd give his life for theirs without question. As strange as it seemed—even to herself—in the midst of a shootout, Deena felt safer than she'd ever had in her entire life.

Deena's pulse pounded in her ears like a herd of stampeding buffalo running free along the plains.

She loved him.

God help her, she loved Asa Grantt.

Instead of fighting his protection, she'd do something for him. Deena tucked SaraGrace more securely into the crook of her arms, making sure as little of her body was as exposed as possible. If Asa would give his life for her, she'd give her life for SaraGrace.

Asa trudged toward their wagon, never stopping despite his struggle. Sweat poured down his near-crimson face. His nostrils flared, and his chest heaved with each ragged breath he expelled.

Rob and Mrs. Paty ran up beside them. Like his brother, Rob did his best to keep her close by his side and shield her with his body.

When they reached the wagon, Asa quickly deposited Deena into the seat, then limped around to the other side. Deena scooted to the middle, making room for the others. Rob helped Mrs. Paty up, then took a step back.

"Get them out of here," Rob said to Asa. "The shooters are retreating. I'm going with the others to track them down."

Asa gave him a curt nod. "Be safe."

Deena could tell Asa wanted to say more. To demand his brother get in the wagon and come with them to safety. But if their roles were reversed, Asa would do the same thing.

Asa cracked the reins, sending the horse off at full gallop into the darkness. The frantic screams of those still trying to make their escape slowly faded until all Deena could hear was the chirp of crickets and call of wild animals.

No one in their small group said anything. What could they say? Ruby Creek was under attack in a whole new way now.

War was officially on the horizon.

Chapter Eighteen

Chickens clucked, cows chomped grass, and horses neighed. Asa barely registered any of it. He sat on his front porch with his revolver, scanning his property for any sign of a disturbance.

After dropping Deena and Mrs. Paty off, then tucking SaraGrace into bed, he'd come out here and hadn't left since. He'd dozed off a time or two for short spells until the nightmares had his eyes popping back open.

Images of Deena and SaraGrace lying in pools of their own blood, bullet holes in their chests or foreheads, kept him vigilant. His leg throbbed. The muscles in his thigh spasmed, drawing taut. Apart from occasionally massaging the sore areas, he did nothing else to ease the pain.

Asa stood when he saw a buggy approaching. His gun stayed lowered, but his finger never left the trigger, in case he needed to execute a quick draw.

His body sagged when Mrs. Paty and Deena came into focus. He glanced down at himself, a new thought finally penetrating the fog of his wariness. He probably looked a fright. His shirt and pants—the ones he hadn't changed out of last night—were wrinkled. The top three buttons of his shirt were undone, revealing a patch of his dark blonde chest hair. His breath probably smelled horrible, and his hair was no doubt a tangled mess from the countless times he'd run his hands through it.

Fixing the only thing he could, he quickly buttoned his shirt and ran his hands over the front in hopes of smoothing out some of the wrinkles. It didn't work.

He walked off the porch and hobbled out to meet them.

Mrs. Paty brought the buggy to a stop, her usual cheerful smile missing. "Good morning, Asa," she said, her weariness evident on her face.

Asa noted her use of his name, instead of one of her terms of endearment. Last night must have taken a tremendous toll on her as well.

"Morning, Mrs. Paty. How are you feeling?" he asked, coming up to the side of the wagon.

She attempted a half-hearted smirk. "Scared. Violated. Angry. I'm just glad no one was hurt last night."

"I agree. Don't worry. We'll figure this out."

She nodded once. Whether or not she believed him or if she was so exhausted that she couldn't muster the energy to care, Asa didn't know.

He helped Deena down and kept her hand in his, needing the connection and reassurance that she was indeed alive and next to him. Sleeplessness and fear had a way of muddling a man's mind.

"Could you bring Deena back tonight?"

"Yes, ma'am. You're welcome to stay with us today if you'd like."

"Thank you, but no. I'd like to get back home."

"Thank you for bringing me here," Deena said.

"Of course. I'm always happy to help where I can."

Asa gave Mrs. Paty's hand a comforting squeeze. "Thank you. Be safe. We're here if you need us."

"I know, dear. You be safe, too." Mrs. Paty headed off.

Asa stood next to Deena, watching her go. "Do you know how to shoot a gun?"

Deena turned her head, studying his profile. "No," she finally answered after a silent beat.

"You're about to learn. Come on." Asa started walking around the house.

"What about the chores? Yes, something dreadful happened last night, but life continues. We let them win if we start neglecting our responsibilities because of fear."

"I told Johnny to handle the big stuff around the farm, and the rest can wait for later. This isn't about being afraid; it's about being prepared."

"I don't think…"

Asa grabbed Deena's shoulders and drew her in, pressing her body against his. He cupped her face, stroking her cheeks with his thumbs, and stared into her eyes. "Nothing is more important than making sure you can defend yourself—especially if I'm not there to protect you."

He bent down and touched his lips to hers. Asa poured his soul into that kiss. Telling her without words how much she meant to him. How broken he'd be if anything bad befell her.

His heart exploded with joy when Deena rose on her toes and kissed him back.

She was his woman. The one given to him to protect, cherish, and honor until his dying breath. He had no doubt about that.

Asa took a step back, breaking the kiss before it went too far. "Are you ready for your shooting lesson now?"

Deena touched a hand to her kiss-swollen lips, a slow smile building on her lovely face. "Yes, sir."

"Good," he said in a weak attempt at sounding composed and stern.

They walked around to the open patch of land behind the house. Earlier that morning, Asa had lined up glass bottles and tin cans on top of the fence posts in preparation for the lesson. He stopped a few feet away from the impromptu targets and pulled out his gun.

"This is a Colt Single Action Army revolver. You don't have to remember the name, but I want you always to remember what it looks like, and how to load and shoot it."

"Colt Single Action Army revolver," Deena repeated. "I'll never forget it."

"Good. Here's how to load it." Asa laid the gun flat in his left palm, for the grip stuck out to the right. "This here is the hammer, the cylinder, and the trigger," he said, pointing to each part in turn. "The ammunition is loaded into the cylinder. Drawing back the hammer rotates the cylinder and loads a new cartridge into the firing position. Pull the trigger to release the hammer and fire the gun."

"Sounds simple enough."

Asa handed the gun to Deena. She gripped the handle and held it away from herself as if she were afraid of shooting off a toe or something equally important. Under different circumstances, he might've laughed.

"I'm gonna show you how to load it. Hold it flat in your hand the way I just did." He waited for her to comply. "Good. This right here is called the gate," he said, pointing to the covering between the back of the cylinder and the hammer. "Open it and pull the hammer back halfway. Great. Load a cartridge in the chamber, then skip one and load the next four chambers."

Deena plucked the five rounds from his hand and loaded them into the gun as he'd instructed. "Why only five, when there is space for six?"

"So that you don't accidentally shoot yourself. Leaving one chamber empty allows the firing pin in the hammer a place to rest. Now, close the gate and pull the hammer all the way back. See how it rotates, and the empty chamber is in front of the hammer."

"Yes. I understand."

"That's the position you always want the chamber in when you're not shooting."

Deena nodded. "Got it."

"Let's practice shooting it. Grip the handle with both hands. Keep the thumb of your right hand on the hammer. Each time before you fire, you'll need to pull it back." He waited for Deena to get a comfortable grasp on the gun and her thumb in place. "Now point it at one the targets. To aim, close one eye and focus the other on the sight at the end of the barrel. That's the fish-fin-looking thing. Line it up with the target. Keep your hands steady and your breathing nice and easy. When you're ready, pull the tiger."

Deena glanced at him, then at the bottles and cans. She closed her left eye and raised the gun. She aimed, taking her time and making adjustments as needed. Finally, she pulled the trigger, sending a bullet flying through the air.

With a loud *tink*, a can exploded, the remnants falling into the grass. Asa's chest swelled with pride, and his worry eased. She was a natural and, at the very least, if she had the time to aim could hit something. They'd worry about fast-paced shooting later.

"Great job. Now, keep going until it's empty."

Deena quickly fired, the rest of the shots missing twice and hitting another can and a bottle. She placed her hands on her hips, examining the remaining targets.

"Not bad. Let's try again. This time, a little farther back."

Asa handed Deena a new set of bullets. She took them and began following the steps he showed her to reload the gun. When she finished, instead of raising the gun and aiming, she turned to face him.

"Asa, this may seem out of the blue, but I have something I need to talk to you about."

Maybe it was the sadness in her eyes or the resolution in her voice like a man standing in front of the hangman's noose saying his final words. Whatever it was, it made Asa not want to hear what Deena had to say next.

"Can it wait until we've practiced a bit more?"

"No, it can't. I lied, Asa, and I need to tell you the truth."

His stomach bottomed out. Sudden confessions after sharing a passionate kiss never boded well for the longevity of a couple's relationship.

"Tell me," he said, steeling himself against what she was about to say.

"I almost don't know where to start."

Asa refrained from making a sarcastic remark about starting from the beginning. Lashing out was a defensive tactic. "Start wherever you're comfortable."

Deena released a long sigh. "I'm not who you think I am. I didn't mean to… Well, I guess I did, but that was before I got to know you. I didn't… I don't want to hurt you. I'm rambling and not making any sense."

Asa stayed quiet, letting her collect her thoughts. So, it was true. Whatever she had to say would hurt him, and likely SaraGrace as well.

"What I'm trying to say is…" she continued.

"Asa! Asa! Come quick," Johnny shouted, cutting off Deena's confession.

They both turned and looked at him as he ran full speed toward them. His frantic expression kept Asa from telling him to come back later. Today was not turning out to be the day for good news.

"What's wrong?" Asa asked when Johnny got closer.

"Two men," he said between gulps of air. He bent over, resting his hands on his knees and catching his breath. "There are two men here to see Deena and you. I spotted them on my way to the stables, snooping around the property. They look like they are up to no good. Especially the one with the white eye and scar running across his face. I told them you were out back, and they said they'd wait for you. They're in the front of the house."

Asa noticed Deena immediately tensed after Johnny described the man. Did she know him? After what happened last night, and the fact that he wasn't expecting any visitors, Asa prepared himself for the worst. He took the revolver from Deena.

"Deena, you go inside with SaraGrace. Johnny, grab the shotgun from my room, then meet me out front."

"Yes, sir," Johnny said, then ran off to do as he'd been told.

"Asa, I don't want you out there alone."

"Johnny will be with me. And please don't argue. Go and stay with SaraGrace. Keep her safe."

Deena rose of her toes and kissed his cheek. "Be safe."

Asa's heart constricted. He was about to lose her. She kissed him as if she were saying goodbye. Even if he survived the two men at his door, he might not survive watching her walk away from him.

Chapter Nineteen

Two men, both wearing three-piece suits and top hats despite the sweltering weather, leaned against a small canopy-covered wagon. Their trousers, slack coats, and matching waistcoats clung perfectly to their frames, denoting the quality and expensiveness of the tailoring. Their clothing was a show of wealth and power.

Too bad for them, for Asa didn't care.

"Mr. Grantt, I presume?" The shorter of the two men asked.

Asa kept his hand on his gun holster. "That's me. Who's asking?"

"My name is Mr. Benjamin Morris of Morris Land Company." He motioned to the tall, thin man with the jagged scar zigzagging across his face through his white left-eye. "This is my associate, Mr. Pete Bloodlow."

Asa eyed Bloodlow. There was a certain kind of savagery to him. As if he were the kind of man who would rob you blind, then break your leg to amuse himself. Morris could possibly blend in with normal society as a proper gentleman. Bloodlow couldn't.

He didn't look, but the open and close of his front door told him that Johnny had come out to stand guard. That put him at ease. A little.

"What can I do for you two?" Asa asked, keeping his tone impassive.

"My associate here is an acquaintance of your intended, Miss Deena Lyon."

"I think you're mistaken. My fiancée's name is Pearl Wilson. Deena is only a nickname." Asa spat at the ground. "Easy mistake."

Morris watched the trail of saliva, his nose wrinkled in disgust. "No mistake. I make it a habit to thoroughly investigate anyone that might affect my business dealings. I assure you, her name is Deena Lyon."

Morris was lying. He had to be. Otherwise, Asa had spent the last few weeks giving his heart to a woman who'd come to scam him. Deena wasn't that kind of person.

What reason did Morris have to lie?

Asa rubbed his stubbled chin. His stomach knotted with dread as a horrible possibility sank in. What if *Deena* was the one lying? After all, she had been about to confess something. And she did mention she lied. Was it about her identity as this man claimed?

"If she's Mr. Bloodlow's acquaintance, what does that have to do with your business?"

"You see, one of my other associates informed me that Deena had come to see him about a certain possession she'd acquired in New York." He pulled out a handkerchief and dabbed at his forehead. "And by acquired, I mean stolen. Naturally, I sought out the owner of the pilfered item to inform them that I knew where to find their property. That quest brought me into Mr. Bloodlow's acquaintance. He so graciously offered me a favor in exchange for the whereabouts of his missing property. So, you see, helping Mr. Bloodlow track down your Deena has put us in league together."

"Enough with the flowery words. Get to the point. What do you want?"

"For you to sell me the deed to your land and your cooperation in helping me obtain the deeds for the rest of the farmlands in Ruby Creek."

Asa's head snapped back. "Excuse me? I must have heard you wrong because it sounded like you said you wanted my land."

The corner of Morris's mouth curled into a sinister sneer. "You did not hear me wrong."

"Why would I ever give you my land?"

Morris's unassuming gentleman persona reappeared. His smile became sugary. "Because if you do, I've convinced Mr. Bloodlow to spare Deena's life."

"Is that a threat?" Asa's hand tightened around his gun.

"Let's call it a choice. Deena's life or your land."

"So, you're the one behind all the stuff that's been happening around here."

"You've been having trouble?"

The wretch had the audacity to look shocked. Bloodlow stood silently next to Morris, an amused grin on his face. Asa's fingers itched to draw his gun and put bullets between both their eyes.

"Good thing I came when I did," Morris continued. "Rumors that an entire town is having trouble with the Indians have a way of driving down property values. Unscrupulous land speculators could swoop in and snatch up your land for next to nothing. Not to worry, I'll give you a fair price."

Asa took a threatening step toward Morris. Like a statue come to life, Bloodlow inserted himself between them.

"You high-binder bottom-feeder," Asa hissed.

"Mr. Grantt," Morris *tsked*, wagging his finger from side to side. "Let's try to keep things civil. For everyone's sake. Take some time to think about my offer. We've traveled in for a short time, so how about we reconvene tomorrow morning? Then, you can give me your final answer."

With a pompous flurry, Morris spun on his heels, giving Asa his back. Bloodlow leaned in close.

Asa stood firm, refusing to cower.

"Think real hard about your decision," Bloodlow said. "Bad things tend to happen to folk out here." He drummed his fingers on the gun in his holster, leaving no room for misunderstanding.

Tipping his hat, Bloodlow turned and climbed into the wagon, next to Morris. They pulled off, leaving Asa fuming in his front yard. He'd have to handle them soon, but first, he now had a more pressing matter to attend to.

***

"Asa, I can explain," Deena said as soon as Asa stormed through the front door. "I don't know what they told you, but I want to tell you the truth."

She held her hands up as if she expected him to charge at her. Asa was so mad that it might not have been such a far-fetched notion if he were a different man. Her eyebrows furrowed, worry marring her enchanting face.

What sickened Asa the most was that even now, knowing that she'd lied and taken advantage of him, he wanted to hug her close until all her troubles faded away.

"How could you expect me to believe anything you have to say, *Deena Lyon*. Where is SaraGrace?"

No matter what was happening between him and Deena, Asa didn't want his daughter witnessing him fussing at the woman she'd come to think of as her new mother.

"I sent her to play in her room."

"Good."

"This is what I was trying to tell you before Johnny ran up."

"Go ahead. Tell me whatever you think you can say to make what you did right."

Deena tried to touch him, but Asa stepped out of her reach. She let her arm fall limp at her side.

"I can't make it right, but I can tell you why I did it." She took a steadying breath, then squared her shoulders, and met his seething glare. "I'm not Pearl Wilson. I was pretending to be her. My name is Deena Lyon. My old master's son Mark gave me that name. Said I was his exotic pet like an African lion. He started taking advantage of me when I was sixteen. I couldn't let him keep hurting me, so I decided to leave.

My mama gave me all the money she'd saved before the war. She'd been planning to buy our freedom but didn't need it anymore. I begged her to come with me up North, but she said she was too old to make the journey. I was swindled out of most of my money by the end of my first week in the city. No one would hire me, and I refused to sell my body, so I started stealing to survive. Got real good at it. Before I came here, I lifted some stuff from Bloodlow. One of those things was a five thousand dollar bearer bond."

Asa's knees wobbled. Her words sucker punched him in the gut. "Five thousand dollars! And you brought that with you here?"

"Yes, but I didn't know what it was," she rushed out.

"What do you mean? Didn't you read it when you stole it?"

Deena broke their eye contact for the first time. She picked at her fingers and said in a small voice, "I don't know how to read. I took the paper to the missionary, Mr. Thompson, at the church and asked him to read it for me. I knew he was lying about what it was, so I asked Mrs. Paty."

Asa raked a hand through his hair. He'd never imagined his frustration and anger could reach such heights. This situation was going from bad to worse.

"What in tarnation? Mrs. Paty knew? You dragged her into this mess?"

"Don't be mad at her. She told me to tell you. I wanted to but I was scared of losing you. Asa, I lov…"

Asa held up a hand, cutting off her declaration. "Don't you dare say that word," he hissed. "I need some air."

Not giving her time to say anything else, Asa stormed from the house and headed to the barn. He needed to blow off some steam, so he could think rationally again. Rage, hurt, and disgust churned inside his gut, making him want to kick, punch, and scream at the heavens.

How could you do this to me, Lord?

He'd thought Deena was the one he could entrust his heart to. The one he'd been afraid he'd never find. A woman who loved him, scars and all.

What a fool he'd been.

Chapter Twenty

"Don't cry, Mama," SaraGrace said, lowering to her knees in front of Deena, who sat on the couch.

Deena had been so consumed by her sorrow that she hadn't heard SaraGrace's approach. She quickly wiped away her tears. Unfortunately, new ones sprang up in their place, making it hard for her to put on a happy face to comfort the little girl she'd come to love as much as she would her own flesh and blood.

"I can't seem to make them stop," Deena said through a watery smile. "But don't worry. I'll be all right."

"Papa is mad at you?"

"Why do you think that?"

"I heard him. He used the voice he uses on me when I'm in trouble."

Deena pulled SaraGrace into her lap and rubbed her back in small, soothing circles. How should she respond? Needless to say, she didn't want her to think her father had done anything wrong.

"Yes, your papa is mad at me."

"Why?"

"Because I lied to him. I didn't tell the truth and that hurt his feelings."

"Why did you lie?"

Innocent, honest questions, but each one pummeled Deena anew. Forcing her to face the ugly truth of her character.

"Because I was selfish. I was in trouble and wanted to protect myself."

SaraGrace's cute little nose wrinkled as she thought about what Deena said. "That's not a bad thing."

"It is when you are willing to hurt other people to protect yourself. We should never hurt other people. Even if they hurt us. I hurt your father—a wonderful man—because I only thought about what I wanted and needed. And now I've hurt you. Made you sad. I'm sorry, SaraGrace."

"It's okay, Mama. I forgive you." SaraGrace hugged Deena with all her strength.

Deena held her closer as more tears welled in her eyes. Just like that, the little girl had absolved her of all her transgressions. No hesitation or conditions. Why couldn't more people do that? Why couldn't she do that with herself?

"Thank you, SaraGrace. I love you so much."

"I love you too, Mama." She drew back from the embrace and wiped Deena's tears. "When Papa comes home, poke out your bottom lip like this when you tell him you're sorry." SaraGrace demonstrated the proper groveling technique. "He'll forgive you if you do it right. He forgives me all the time."

A snort of laughter bubbled up Deena's throat and erupted from her mouth. She could point out that the reason Asa so easily caved to such under-handed tactics was SaraGrace was both his daughter and absurdly adorable. Two advantages Deena did not possess. But she couldn't bring herself to squash the little girl's hopes of helping mend the rift between Asa and her.

"That sounds like a grand idea. Thank you for sharing it."

SaraGrace gave her a toothy grin. "You're welcome. So, are you done crying now?"

"Yes, I am."

"Good. I don't like seeing you cry. Want to play dolls with me?"

"That sounds lovely."

"Let me get them. I'll be right back."

Deena watched SaraGrace dash off to her room. She'd miss her something fierce. Asa would never bad-mouth her to SaraGrace, but Deena wondered what he'd tell her about why she was gone.

The thought of Asa sending her packing tore Deena up. It was the least she deserved, though. If he didn't call the sheriff on her, that would be a blessing. Either way, she'd wait for him to come back and deliver his verdict. Because for the first time in a long time, she was tired of running from her problems.

She'd no longer be a coward. From now on, Deena Lyon would be a woman who faced her troubles and whatever consequences that came with them.

***

Asa slung his ax overhead and brought it down on the hunk of wood with a dense thunk. The wood split in two, each half falling into the piles on either side of the tree stump he used as a chopping block.

His arms burned from repeating the action countless times in the last half-hour. It had served its purpose, though. He'd thought long and hard about what he wanted to do and was pretty certain he'd made up his mind.

He rocked the handle up and down to wedge it out of the tree stump. Two more pieces, then he'd go inside and have another conversation with Deena. Asa picked up another log and placed it in the middle of the tree stump. Before he could swing the ax, a rider came tearing toward him, their horse running at full speed.

Asa waited until the rider came closer. It was Rob. He lodged the ax in the stump, then sat down and took a swig of water from his canteen while he waited for his brother to stop.

Raising a hand to keep the sun out of his eyes, he looked at Rob atop his mount. "Keep riding like that, and you're going to trip your horse and break your neck."

"Mr. Baile is dead," Rob stated without preamble. "They found him on the edge of town scalped, and his throat slit."

Asa closed his eyes. Those bastards. "I know who did it." He opened his eyes, meeting his brother's stunned gaze.

Rob jumped from his saddle, landing next to him. "How? Who was it?"

"Two men by the names Benjamin Morris and Pete Bloodlow paid me a visit this morning." Asa rolled his shoulders, trying to dispel the tension drawing his muscles taut.

"And? What's the rest of it? You know what I'm gonna ask next. Tell me the whole story."

"Deena isn't Pearl. She's a pickpocket from New York that somehow found out about me and Pearl's arrangement. She came here because she was running from Bloodlow. He's some kind of outlaw in that city. She stole a five thousand dollar bearer bond from him."

"Five thousand dollars!" Rob whistled.

"Yup. He was out to kill her for it. Guess she thought she could hide out here since we're so far away from New York."

Rob crossed his arms, his expression thoughtful as he tried to fit all the pieces together. "How'd he figure out she was here?"

"She can't read. She went to the missionary Mr. Thompson to have him read the paper to her. He told his boss Mr. Morris and…" Asa went still. "That's it!"

"What's what?"

Asa sprang up with more nimbleness than he'd been able to employ in a long time. "The missionary. That's how we prove it was them. Morris said an associate of his told him about Deena. Thompson is the missionary she went to, so he must be working for Morris, who has been causing all our trouble since he wants us to sell him our land. If we get the missionary to talk, he could give us what we need to show it was Morris and Bloodlow."

"Are you sure it's Thompson? Did Morris say he was the associate?"

"No, but Deena said she went to him to read the bearer bond. Hold on. Come with me." Asa took off toward his house.

He found Deena in SaraGrace's room, lying on her stomach on the floor, playing dolls. His heart squeezed at the sight. They almost looked like a real mother and daughter, happily enjoying each other's company.

Asa cleared his throat, getting their attention. "Deena, I need you to answer me truthfully."

She sat up and gave him her full attention. "Yes, of course."

"The man that came to see me. His name was Benjamin Morris. He owns Morris Land Company."

"Morris Land Company? That doesn't sound familiar."

"He said that his associate told him you had the bond. I think that the associate is Mr. Thompson. Is he the only person you showed the bond to, besides Mrs. Paty?"

"Yes. He's the only one." She snapped her fingers, then pointed at Asa. "When I went to the church, there was a map with the name Ruby

Creek printed at the top, laying across one of the benches. I made sure to memorize those two words before I came here so I could recognize them if I needed to for any reason. There were also three more words on the map."

"Can you write what those three words looked like?"

"I think so. I can recreate what I saw."

Asa scrambled to get her a piece of paper and a pencil. Deena slowly traced out the three words she'd seen.

Morris Land Company.

Rob and Asa exchanged knowing looks.

"Rob, I need you to stay here and look after Deena and SaraGrace for me," Asa said, already making his way out of the room. "I'll go get the sheriff, and we'll go talk to Mr. Thompson."

"Anything you need, brother."

"Thank you."

Deena followed him from the room. He didn't pull away when she touched his arm.

"Asa, please be careful."

Asa searched her face. The concern seemed genuine, a fact that exhilarated and saddened him. He didn't know what he'd be facing in the next few hours. Morris and Bloodlow had proven themselves to be dangerous. This could very well be the last time he saw her, and there was so much left unsaid between them.

There wasn't time to say it all, so he said nothing. Asa nodded, then headed out the door.

Chapter Twenty-One

Asa crept along the side of the church with his gun drawn. Sheriff Griffin walked behind him, his gun still in the holster. For all his prancing about town puffing out his barrel chest as he boasted about how he'd put the fear of God in all the outlaws for miles around, it had been like pulling teeth getting the man to come along.

"Are you sure about this?" Sheriff Griffin asked. "Mr. Thompson is a man of God. I've had a drink with him a time or two at the saloon. Seems like an upstanding fellow. Accusing someone of murder isn't a small thing."

If he didn't know any better, Asa would have guessed that the quaver in the sheriff's voice meant he was scared. At least he had the good sense to whisper.

"Yes, I'm sure. And we're only going to talk to him."

"Then, why do you have your gun drawn?"

Asa didn't have time for this. Either the sheriff would come with him, or he wouldn't. No matter what the other man did, his family's lives were in danger, and he'd get to the bottom of this one way or another.

"I'll go first," Asa said over his shoulder.

He rounded the corner of the building and inched toward the front door. Standing next to the door, he called out, "Mr. Thompson, it's Asa Grantt. I came to ask you a few questions."

No response came at first. Then, there was some shuffling and a loud thud. Sheriff Griffin finally pulled out his gun.

"Help," a man inside the church called out. "He's trying to kill me."

Asa busted through the door. At the front of the church, Bloodlow was tossing the benches aside, his gun drawn and pointed at the man crawling beneath them.

Asa aimed and fired. He missed.

Bloodlow glared at Asa, his top lip curled into a vicious snarl. He slammed the hammer of his revolver right after pulling the trigger to shoot three rapid-fire shots. Asa dived to the side, but not fast enough. A shot grazed his shoulder, causing searing pain to shoot through his arm.

Where is the sheriff?

Asa glanced back at the doorway. There was no one there. He was on his own.

He lay on his side and shot at Bloodlow's feet. He missed, then hit Bloodlow's shin, sending him crashing to the ground. Asa rolled into a sitting position and fired again.

Bloodlow rolled behind an overturned bench, finding protection from the shot. Asa fired again, hitting the bench. Bloodlow peeked from behind the barrier and fired back, missing Asa by a good distance.

Moving fast, Asa aimed at Bloodlow's exposed upper body, then pulled the trigger. His gun clicked, but nothing happened. He checked the cylinder. Empty.

Chariots of fire!

Bloodlow hobbled to his feet and stalked toward Asa, his gun drawn.

Asa stood, his head held high, never taking his eyes off Bloodlow. If today were the day he died, he'd meet that death with dignity.

"How dare you shoot me," Bloodlow snarled. "After I kill you, I'm going to have fun taking care of your woman and daughter, you yellow-belly…"

A shot sped from the back of the church and hit Bloodlow in the chest. He clutched the front of his shirt, blood seeping through his fingers.

He collapsed on the floor, a string of gurgled curses on his lips. He twitched for several minutes, then went still, his glassy eyes staring straight ahead.

Asa looked over his shoulder and found Deena standing in the doorway, her gun still aimed where Bloodlow had stood.

"Deena?"

She started as if the sound of her name had pulled her from a trance. Asa ran up to her and folded her in a firm embrace.

"What were you thinking? You followed me here?"

She drew back and ran her hands over his face as if reassuring herself that he was indeed alive and still here with her. "I saw that sheriff when I came into town before. I knew he wouldn't be much help. I had to do something."

"You could have gotten hurt."

"I could say the same to you."

Behind them, footsteps echoed across the wood floor, followed by a loud gasp.

"Gracious. You killed a man," the sheriff said, his voice shakier than before. He walked further into the church, dragging Mr. Thompson by the arm.

"That's Bloodlow," Asa said nodding toward him. "The man I was telling you about. The one who showed up on my land threatening my family. He shot first and I had to defend myself."

"It's true," Mr. Thompson said. "Bloodlow started this. He tried to kill me and Asa saved me."

"I see. Well, I'm sorry I couldn't help Asa. I had to go out and apprehend Mr. Thompson before he ran away."

Asa shook his head. No doubt those two were outside holding each other while they cowered behind a tree.

"I understand," Asa replied, sarcasm in every word. He sauntered up to Mr. Thompson, his hand on his gun. It was empty, but the other man didn't know that. "Start talking," he ordered.

"Thank you. Thank you for saving me. I didn't kill Mr. Baile. Bloodlow did that. Mr. Morris hired me to cause a little trouble here and there, but that's all I did. The attack on the barn dance was Bloodlow, and some hired guns. Mr. Baile knew it was me stirring things up and was planning to tell everyone. When I told Morris, he had him killed."

"How do we know you're not lying?" Asa tapped a finger against his holster.

Mr. Thompson watched the action. He swallowed, his face turning ghostly pale. He fanned himself.

"Bloodlow stole a necklace off Baile. One the Indians gave to him. He wanted to keep it as a trophy. Check his belongings, and you'll find it."

"It's true," Deena said. "Last time I saw Mr. Baile at Alice's shop, he had a necklace on that Chief Struck by the Ree had given him."

"Fine," the sheriff said as if he'd been in charge of this interrogation the entire time. "We'll search for the necklace. If we find it, you testify against Morris, and I'll talk to the judge on your behalf."

"Thank you." Mr. Thompson bowed his head and folded his hands in front of him as if he were praying. He should have been doing a little more of that before he got himself tied up with Morris and his seedy lot.

"I'll send someone around to fetch the body and send him to the coroner," Sheriff Griffin said, already yanking Mr. Thompson toward the door.

His bluish-green coloring and the way he kept lifting his hand under his nose suggested he wasn't comfortable in their current situation. Asa watched him hurry off. How a man who was uneasy around a dead body became the sheriff of a town in the West was beyond him.

"Come on let's step outside," Asa said, taking Deena by the elbow and following the sheriff out. Once they were outside, the gruesome scene behind them, he took her hands. "How are you feeling?"

"I killed him," she replied in a flat tone.

"Yes, you did."

"Would it be wrong of me to say I'm not sorry about it? I'm not saying he deserved it, but he tried to hurt you. I'd defend you again any day."

"I understand. That's not wrong, but it can be hard on a person. How are you feeling?"

"I'd like to go home."

"Then let's go."

Asa gathered Deena to his side and walked with her over to the hitching post where they'd tied their horses. She placed her hand over his before he could untie the reins.

"Wait. I have to say this. Asa, I don't expect you to forgive me. I'll never forgive myself for bringing this trouble to your door. But I love you, and I couldn't live with myself if something happened to you."

"I love you too, Deena."

"What?"

Asa smiled wide, his boundless joy refusing to be contained. "I said 'I love you.'"

"Asa, I…"

He touched a finger to Deena's lips. "Forgiveness is a tricky thing. In order to give it, we have to be hurt by someone, which of course, makes us want to close ourselves off. But when we do that, we don't acknowledge the fact that people can learn and grow past their mistakes. I've hurt people in the past, and as much as I hate to think about it, one day, I'll probably do something to hurt you. I can't accept forgiveness from others if I'm not willing to give it myself. So, if you'll have me, I'd like to make you my wife."

"Yes! Yes, I'll have you, Asa Grantt."

Asa leaned Deena back and pressed his lips to hers, kissing her soundly. She laughed into his lips, then wrapped her arms around his neck and kissed him back.

When they pulled apart, Deena stroked the side of his face. "Thank you for loving me."

"Thank you for teaching me how to love more fully."

Asa wanted to crow from the highest mountain. Deena Lyon was officially his woman. They would walk this earth together until the Lord called them home.

Once they were alone, Asa laced his fingers through Deena's. "So, what are we going to do now?"

"We're going home to get SaraGrace, then head to the next town over to get married."

"Right now?" Deena's eyes gleamed with excitement.

Asa lifted their joined hands and kissed her knuckles. "Yes. We're short a minister in Ruby Creek now, and I'm not wasting another second making you my wife."

"Well then, what are we waiting for? Daylight's a'wastin'."

Chapter Twenty-Two

Two weeks later

Paradise. Utopia. Heaven. Whatever name Deena used to describe the current state of her life, one thing remained the same: she wouldn't change a single thing about it.

Two blissful weeks after marrying Asa and he still looked at her every morning as if she were the greatest gift he'd ever been given. And she spent every hour of the day showing him how much she appreciated having him in her life.

They sat on the porch in their rocking chairs, holding hands and watching the sunset, as had become their habit every evening.

"I was thinking," Asa said. "How about we buy an Arabian as well?"

Deena thought about that for a moment. "Arabians are beautiful horses as well. Fast too. We'd make a good profit raising them."

"Is that a yes?"

"Only if Juniper and Jasper don't mind sharing the stables."

Asa snorted. "I'm sure they'll be fine with it. And if not, I'll get our horse-whisperer to talking them into it."

"Is that what we're calling SaraGrace now?"

"The girl has a natural talent."

"Very true." Deena squeezed her husband's hand, a contented smile on her lips.

After everything had been squared away with Bloodlow and Morris, she and Asa had gone down to the sheriff's office to talk to him about the bond she'd stolen. By law, a bear bond had no registered owner. It belonged to whoever was holding it, which was why it was so highly favored by outlaws.

Since Deena had it, she owned it. She and Asa had quickly cashed it and built a brand-new corral, updated the stables, and purchased two Friesian horses—Jasper and Juniper.

Giving Asa his dream of becoming a horse breeder was as much a gift for Deena as it had been for him.

Deena sat up in her chair when she spotted a wagon off in the distance, headed their way.

"Are we expecting visitors?" she asked Asa.

"Not that I'm aware."

They waited for the wagon to get closer, then rose and walked down the porch to meet whoever had come calling. Deena's chest tightened and her heart jumped into her throat when the wagon came to a stop, and two familiar faces hopped out.

Mrs. Crenshaw and Pearl Wilson.

"Good evening, ladies," Asa said, unaware of who they were. "May we help you with something? We weren't expecting any visitors tonight."

The older of the two women stepped forward, extending her arm. She shook with Asa, then stepped back next to her companion. "My name is Mrs. Milly Crenshaw, and this is Miss. Pearl Wilson."

"Oh…" Asa scratched his head. His mouth opened and closed several times, but he didn't say anything else. His face was as white as cotton.

"I'm Deena Grantt, and this is my husband, Asa." Deena didn't extend her hand, opting to do a small curtsy, in case Miss. Wilson carried a grudge she wanted to take out physically. "How about we all go inside and talk?"

"That sounds like a wonderful idea."

Deena grabbed Asa's hand and led the way inside. This was not how she'd envisioned her night ending, but it was for the best. It was past time she made amends with Pearl.

***

"Well," Mrs. Crenshaw said after taking a sip of the coffee Deena had served. "I do believe we all know why Miss.. Wilson and I are here, so how about we discuss why Deena is now Mrs. Grantt and not Pearl?"

Deena scooted to the edge of her chair and faced Pearl. "First, I'd like to apologize to you, Pearl. I can never make right what I did to you, but I am truly sorry. The day you two met at the restaurant in New York City a few weeks back, I was sitting at the next table. I didn't mean to at first, but I overheard your conversation about coming out to marry Asa."

"Which also means you heard the part where I couldn't come because I was taking care of my *ailing* grandmother," Pearl snapped. She lifted her nose in the air. "What kind of person does a thing like that?"

Deena flinched as if those words were a physical blow. The pain they caused her certainly made it feel like they were. So Pearl wasn't mad—she was furious. Deena didn't begrudge her for that. She had every right to be.

"A terrible, desperate, scared person. Again, I know this doesn't make it right, but I was in a lot of trouble at that time."

"I bet you were. A low-life criminal like you is probably involved in all kinds of seedy activities."

Asa placed a hand on Deena's shoulder. "I understand that you're upset, but I won't have you talking to my wife like that."

"But she…"

"I agree," Mrs. Crenshaw said. "I didn't bring you here to get revenge. Only closure."

Pearl crossed her arms, her murderous scowl cutting Deena to the bone. "Fine, then. You were in trouble, so you stole my future, and now you're sorry for it. What am I supposed to do with that?"

"Hopefully, understand and move on with your life," Asa said. "I'm not defending my wife's actions. What she did was wrong. But Deena isn't that person anymore. I truly hope one day you heal from this and find the man the Lord has in store for you. That man isn't me. He brought Deena and me together and 'what the Lord has put together, let no man put asunder.'"

"Very well said," Mrs. Crenshaw said. "I started my agency because the Lord put it on my heart to help settle the West by finding brides for the brave men who've come out here to stake their claim. If this is His will, so be it. It's a bit unorthodox, but the Lord works in mysterious ways."

"Yes, He does," Deena said, holding back her mirth.

She looked at her husband. In her mind, this was never meant to be her future. People like her weren't supposed to find love, family, and good friends. The Lord had opened her world to brand new possibilities through Asa, and for that, she would be forever grateful.

A loud knock sounded on the door before it burst open. Rob sauntered into the house, his usual infectious smile illuminating his face.

"Evening, family. I…" he started, then stopped when he noticed the two women. His eyes locked on Pearl and never looked away. "Oh, beg your pardon. I didn't know you had guests. And such captivating guests, at that."

A soft blush dotted Pearl's cheeks. She touched a hand to her mouth and batted her lashes in a demure gesture.

"My name is Rob Grantt. Brother to this whippersnapper." He thumbed in Asa's direction. "And who might you be, darlin'?"

Deena glanced at Asa. They both covered their mouths with their fists to suppress their laughter. It looked like Pearl might not have long to wait before nabbing her husband.

Mysterious ways, indeed.

Dear Reader,

The wild days of the Old West were a truly fascinating time period. I enjoyed learning about this period so much and feel like I've barely scratched the surface of the richness of that era. Men and women left everything behind in the hopes of creating a new life for themselves. It wasn't easy, but the men and women who stuck it out had true grit.

I hope you have enjoyed reading Deena & Asa's story as much as I have enjoyed being the vessel through which it was presented to you.

I love hearing from readers. Feel free to drop me a line at **info@authorgscarr.com**, to ask questions, or gush with me about the books, what you had for breakfast, your favorite cat meme, whatever.

Again, thank you so much for reading. I am literally nothing without you.

Until the next story,

G.S. Carr

<u>Other books by Author G.S. Carr</u>

The Cost of Love Series:
The Cost of Hope
The Cost of Atonement
The Cost of Rebellion

Ladies of the Civil War Series:
Lady of Secrets
Lady of Disguise – August 2020
Lady of Healing - Coming fall 2020
Lady of Faith - Coming winter 2020

Westward Home & Hearts Mail-Order Brides Series:
Deena's Deception
Anna's answer – August 2020

Keep in touch:
www.gscarr.com
www.facebook.com/authorgscarr
Instagram: @authorgscarr
info@authorgscarr.com

www.ingramcontent.com/pod-product-compliance
Lightning Source LLC
Chambersburg PA
CBHW021955120726
47992CB00001B/262